LANDRA JENNINGS

Clarion Books
An Imprint of HarperCollins*Publishers*

Clarion Books is an imprint of HarperCollins Publishers.

Library of Congress Cataloging-in-Publication Data
Names: Jennings, Landra, author.
Title: Wand / Landra Jennings.
Description: First edition. | New York : Clarion Books, [2023] | Audience: Ages 8-12.
| Audience: Grades 4-6. | Summary: Eleven-year-old Mira meets a mysterious girl
who grants her three wishes, but when none bring Mira the sense of belonging
she is looking for, she ventures into another world to find her true family.
Identifiers: LCCN 2022045239 | ISBN 9780358674573 (hardcover)
Subjects: CYAC: Grief--Fiction. | Magic--Fiction. | Wishes--Fiction. | Belonging--
Fiction. | Orphans--Fiction. | Fantasy. | LCGFT: Fantasy fiction. | Novels.
Classification: LCC PZ7.1.J4536 Wan 2023 | DDC [Fic]--dc23
LC record available at https://lccn.loc.gov/2022045239

Typography by Marcie Lawrence
23 24 25 26 27 LBC 5 4 3 2 1

First Edition

For John, Thomas, and Will

Chapter One

Something watched from the kitchen window.

Mira noticed it peering in as she gathered the ingredients for the pancakes.

The others didn't seem to notice. Ten-year-old Sara waltzed around in her pajamas and a pair of yellow sunglasses missing the lenses. Sara's four-year-old little sister, Beans, sat kicking the table, fully decked out in green knee socks and the pink princess dress she'd been wearing for a week. Val was on the phone, leafing through mail and doing a lot of sighing.

It was a bird with golden feathers and a pointed bill, perched in the mulberry tree outside. Mira felt its stare whenever she passed the window. She'd never seen a bird like that before.

Val put a hand over the phone. "Thanks so much for cooking again, Mira."

Mira gave a little jump and nodded. It was impressive, she knew, being in charge of the pancakes when she was only eleven.

Val didn't say anything more to Mira; she went back to her conversation, holding the phone between her chin and shoulder while she pulled her long blond hair into its typical ponytail. She wore her Shampooch Palace T-shirt. She'd be leaving for work soon.

"I want honey on mine," Beans said, adjusting the headband of silver stars that was nestled in her curls. "Pixies love you if you smell like honey."

Mira blinked, forgetting about the bird for a moment. "There's no such thing as pixies. And *you* love chocolate chips, remember? Chocolate chips are our special Saturday morning tradition."

"Our charming tradition," Sara interjected chirpily. Her cheerfulness had a forced note, as it often did. She wielded an imaginary sword, miming a poke at Val, who waved her away.

"Tradition is dumb." Beans's *r*'s often sounded like *w*'s, especially if she was upset. *Twadition.*

"Would you like to help me with the pancakes?" Mira said.

Beans came alert and hopped down to shove her chair over to the counter; the chair legs scraped loudly against the floor tile.

A flash of gold in the window. The rushing of wings. The bird, leaving. Maybe the noise had startled it. Mira felt an unexplainable relief.

She steadied the chair while Beans climbed up to stand on the seat. Beans was such a small girl, with short, delicate limbs, like her mom and sister. She insisted she didn't need any help now that she was four, but she weighed almost nothing. If she fell, Mira could easily catch her.

Beans took an egg in her small fingers, cracked it against the side of the bowl, then proceeded to dump the yolk, the whites, and most of the shell inside.

Mira wanted to roll her eyes, but Beans would have noticed. "Excellent work," Mira said, and fished out the shell bits with a spoon. She guided Beans in using the nonstick spray can. Beans coated the griddle as well as a generous portion of the wall behind the stove.

Mira sponged off the wall, glanced at Val to see if she was admiring how helpful Mira was being (Val wasn't), then poured dollops of batter onto the griddle. She showed Beans how to wait for the tops to bubble, how to use the turner. The scent of melting chocolate filled the air.

Val went into the family room next to the kitchen and began whispering into the phone.

What was it about whispering that caused you to listen harder? Mira caught a few words like *expensive* and *extra hours*, and her stomach twisted. Val had taken Mira to It's Fashion last week because she was outgrowing all of her clothes. Mira's heart had dropped at the total on the register, and she didn't mention she needed new shoes too—the only shoes that still fit her were flip-flops. Was Val talking about how much the clothes had cost?

Mira and Beans finished making the pancakes, and Val appeared in the kitchen doorway. "Can you watch the girls tomorrow afternoon, Mira? At the library? I'm going to help Abbie." Abbie owned a cleaning service. If she had an apartment move-in or move-out on a day when Shampooch Palace was closed, she often asked Val for help.

Again? Mira thought. But she turned her lips up into a

3

quick smile and nodded before nibbling at her breakfast. She focused on the warmth of the pancake on her tongue, along with the sweetness of the syrup, trying to bring back that special Saturday-morning feeling she used to get when Papa was still here. Then she put the dishes in the dishwasher and walked on her toes—a habit left over from gymnastics—into the family room, where Val was rummaging in her purse.

Mira ran her fingers over the smooth leather of the recliner that'd once been Papa's. No one really wanted that chair anymore. These days they mostly used it to hold laundry. It was just an extra thing no one knew what to do with, that chair. A random old thing that was just *still here.*

Like me, Mira thought. A lump formed in her throat, and she reached for the pendant on her necklace. The opaque emerald-green stone reminded Mira of a fig beetle and always felt warm. But sometimes even the warmth of the pendant didn't provide comfort. A wave of sadness washed over her.

Val was jamming her feet into her work shoes without untying the laces; she glanced up. "Everything okay?"

No, Mira thought. But she reminded herself of what Val had done, the horrible thing she had done on that terrible day, and why Mira could *never ever* forgive her. A familiar heat flooded Mira's chest. It dried up all the sadness. She cleared her throat. "Yes, everything's fine."

The doorbell rang and Val hurried to answer.

Some instinct made Mira glance out the window that faced

the back porch. Even at that distance, she could see the bird in the magnolia tree. It hadn't flown off; it'd only moved from the front yard to the back, its golden presence unmistakable. Though she would have thought it difficult to see her from that far away, and through a sheer curtain no less, it *did* seem to be watching. Not foraging, not building a nest, just watching.

That bird was too big, too bright, too strange. It didn't fit in around here any better than Mira did. What was it doing here? Where had it come from?

Chapter Two

Glass Pond wasn't any good for swimming. Mira knew that. Everyone in Between, Georgia, knew that.

And even if they hadn't, they wouldn't have been able to try it out for themselves. The pond behind the Marathon gas station was locked up tight, surrounded by a tall wooden fence someone had painted black and fronted by a collection of cypress and holly trees interwoven with vines. The gate wasn't operable—or didn't seem to be; there wasn't a latch in view. *No Admittance* signs were plastered everywhere.

Of course, all that trying to keep people *out* just made some people want to get *in*. But the occasional hooligan reported the gate wouldn't budge, the fence was full of sharp splinters, and the shrubbery was host to countless copperheads and yellow jackets just waiting to get ahold of whoever tried to penetrate the tangle.

Mrs. Martha, who worked at the Between Grocery attached to the gas station, was quick to warn anyone who would listen about the danger. She wasn't sure who owned the property, she said, but whoever they were, they didn't do enough caretaking.

She whispered about some people who had drowned there, once upon a time, and laughed off the more outlandish rumors, rumors that were bound to circulate in a town where there wasn't quite enough to occupy everyone's time.

The rumors *were* of the ridiculous sort—even Papa had said so: how Glass Pond supposedly led to someplace *else*. How it vomited up the strange characters who appeared randomly, confused and disoriented, in the gas station parking lot. How the odd people clearly weren't from around here and probably weren't from anywhere on Earth. I mean, look at them! A man with a mustache on his forehead who sang for quarters. A woman in purple pantaloons who claimed a snake lived in her nose (no one had actually confirmed this). A bald individual who kept asking people to pick a card from a very peculiar deck. *Those* types of people surely must've gotten sucked through Glass Pond from elsewhere—otherwise why would they have ended up in the nowhere town of Between, of all places?

Mrs. Martha would cheekily claim that souls certainly came from *all* over to sample the chicken and biscuits she cooked up for to-go lunches at the Between Grocery. That she was out-of-this-world famous. And the townspeople would laugh and agree that the strange people must have come from far afield to sample her legendary fare, though the rumors were more fun to think about.

* * *

The babysitter, Mrs. Sutter, loved to talk about Glass Pond. In fact, Mrs. Sutter claimed to be something of an expert in the doings of the pond. However, Mira, Sara, and Beans had already heard all of her theories because the woman came over a *lot*.

Up until a year ago, Mrs. Sutter had been merely the crabby old lady next door, the one Papa and Gammy hadn't liked, the one with the white hair, bottle-thick glasses, and habit of going out with a baseball bat whenever unfamiliar cars drove by. But when Val decided to add more days to her weekly work schedule and eliminate Mira's and Sara's after-school activities, she'd gotten more desperate than ever for babysitters, and somehow Mrs. Sutter convinced Val she was perfect for the job.

That Saturday afternoon, Mrs. Sutter was at their house again, as usual. She was also making Mira miserable, as usual. That was because Mrs. Sutter's *second*-favorite topic of discussion was Mira: she slouched too much, she frowned too often, she didn't *make enough of an effort to be pleasant*.

Mrs. Sutter sat heavily on the sofa, fixing her gaze on Mira.

Mira sank deeper into Papa's recliner, holding her book—*Orphan Island*—a little higher, hoping the woman would take the hint.

"Them that come out of Glass Pond are rude like you," Mrs. Sutter said. "Them that's magic think they know what's what."

The woman was going to get up and collect Mira's book soon, Mira knew. *You look your elders in the eye, young lady.*

Mira wondered why Mrs. Sutter didn't prey on the others instead of her. She put her book down and tried to make her voice respectful. "I like to read. It's good for you." Papa had always said it.

"You think you're so smart, don't you?" Mrs. Sutter said. "Smarter than the others, at least in your own high-and-mighty mind. Probably think you're going to college." And her lips pursed into a tiny, satisfied smile, like she knew something Mira didn't.

Mira hadn't given any thought to college. She shrugged and studied the carpet, trying to figure out how to escape. She'd be upstairs in the attic if it wasn't so stifling this time of day.

"Val ought to get a medal, putting up with you and your attitude," Mrs. Sutter said.

Mira didn't believe she had an attitude. But arguing with Mrs. Sutter accomplished nothing.

"You ought to be thankful Val keeps you here at all," Mrs. Sutter said. "You're no kin to her. *I* sure wouldn't have you. Not a thankless girl like you. Let's just hope your meager efforts are enough."

Mira's face was getting hot. She stood. "I've got to, um, go." Unfortunately, Mrs. Sutter raised her voice and, even when Mira was in the bathroom, she could hear the woman talking about how Mira wasn't nearly grateful enough for her many blessings.

Mira shoved a rolled towel into the crack at the bottom of the door and tried making herself comfortable on the bathmat with her book, but found her arms shook and the page was blurry and she couldn't read a word.

When Mrs. Sutter first told Mira last year that Val only kept Mira around to be useful, Mira had wanted to ask Val about it, but for some reason hadn't been able to get the question out of her lips.

Instead, Mira tested the theory. One Sunday, she'd washed Beans's clothes in addition to her own, vacuumed the family room, and weeded the front walk. At the end of that day, Val *was* much happier. She smiled for the first time in a week, praised Mira for her good work, and started consulting her on the grocery list. It was important Mira earn her keep, she'd realized. She *needed* to be useful. Like it or not, that was her role in the house these days.

Mira put her book down, wiped her eyes, and took a deep breath. She retrieved the Comet cleanser and a scrub brush from beneath the sink and began a vigorous attack on the tub.

* * *

That night, Mira had a dream she'd been having frequently. She was on the balance beam, doing the big-arms toe-touch routine she'd done on the floor beam when she was first learning gymnastics. Only, the beam wasn't on the floor. The beam seemed to be somewhere in space—there was just darkness below her, a swirling, fathomless depth. And she carried heavy suitcases in each hand as she carefully placed her feet, suitcases that were somehow terribly important, although she didn't know what was in them. Her arms were straining, straining, trying to hold the suitcases up and out from her body. Sweat poured down her face.

She was going to lose her balance, she felt, at any minute. And then she would fall.

Chapter Three

When Mira was nine, a fledgling crow had appeared one morning outside her bedroom window, abandoned on the sill. A day passed and the bird's parents didn't come to claim it. The young bird began to look feeble, staring in at her. She put out boiled eggs and cooked oatmeal like Papa suggested, and the crow soon perked up.

Bandit still lived in the woods nearby. Mira never knew when he would come around. Or what he would try to take when he did. He came by his name naturally.

One week, it was wiper blades. Mira would see him flying by, floppy blades hanging from his bill. She didn't know which cars he raided. Another time, it was small metal objects like keys, screws, or toys. Beans had to move her Hot Wheels collection inside for safekeeping. Lately, Bandit was obsessed with anything that looked like a stick. It had gotten so bad, Mira couldn't do her homework on the picnic table without him suddenly appearing from nowhere to make a great swoop for her pencil.

True, Bandit was a bit of a thief. But he also took it upon

himself to warn Mira of dangerous things. Naturally, they were things the *crow* considered dangerous, not necessarily the things Mira did. It often took some time for her to locate the source of his distress: an owl roosting in a tree nearby; a dozen fake crows a neighbor had put out for Halloween decor; a particularly aggressive display of balloons, hung to celebrate someone's graduation.

That Sunday morning it was the strange bird that Bandit was concerned about.

From a high branch in the magnolia tree, the bird's golden feathers glowed in the morning light.

Mira was sitting on the flat rock beside the sandbox. "I see him, Bandit. It's okay."

Bandit, in the nearby maple tree, grumbled, but his ruffled feathers smoothed.

Mira had a way with animals. Papa had often commented on it. Not only Bandit, but the other birds, the rabbits, deer, and even the foxes, who would let their pups venture into her yard to have their fuzzy heads rubbed. She held out a hand for the strange bird. "Come on," she said. "I wouldn't hurt you."

But the bird just turned his golden head this way and that, inspecting her from one eye and then the other, making no move to come closer.

Mira let her arm drop. "That's all right. I'm sure Bandit would prefer you stay away."

Bandit seemed to agree. He issued a few last threatening caws. The lack of response must've convinced him he'd made his point. He lost interest and flew into the woods.

Mira returned her gaze to the sky, savoring the orange-red remnants of the dawn and studying the clouds floating overhead. The cloud with the swirly edges looked like a castle, she decided. A castle loaded with mysterious gabled towers and secret passageways.

Papa had once talked about adding a castle to Fairy Village.

He'd built the village supposedly for the pixies, but it had really been for Mira's Bratz, Barbie, and troll dolls. He drywalled the miniature buildings with bark, built roofs from twigs, and installed ornate doors ordered from catalogs. The village took up the entire section of yard between the magnolia tree and the neighbor's fence. These days, Mira didn't play with dolls but still weeded the village paths, cleaned the buildings, and repaired the tiny furniture with floral wire, imitating Papa's efforts as best she could.

"Top of the morning to you," she said to the village. It was a little exchange she and Papa used to do, along with clapping and turning three times and calling for the pixies.

Only the rustling of the wind in the trees answered her. Not Papa, who had always answered for the pixies in a high, squeaky voice, "And the rest of the day to you."

The morning seemed to sour. How silly she was. She was far too old to say "Top of the morning" to doll villages.

She stood and brushed off her shorts. Dropping into a handstand, she turned the world upside down, her pendant gently bumping against her chin, the grass soft against her palms. She took a deep breath, and then she popped gracefully upright again. There was no one to appreciate the maneuver except . . .

The golden bird was now directly in front of her, perched on the fence. He was bigger than she'd first thought, bigger than the crow, with a short tail. He leered down a long bill at her and unfolded a crest—which had been lying flat on his head—into a large violet fan, like he was showing off a particularly audacious hat.

"Oh," Mira said, surprised. None of the other birds around her house had crests like that.

The bird opened that large bill and let out a scream.

Mira jumped a mile. The call had definitely been a scream, not a happy sound. And it had sounded like a shout of *Here!* Like the bird had found Mira out in a game of hide-and-seek or had caught her doing something she oughtn't.

"*What* are you so upset about?" Mira said, her heart pounding.

"There you are," someone said.

An older girl, maybe fifteen, was inside the woods. She was taller than Mira but not by much. The girl had a braid the color of wild plums, mysterious older-girl makeup on her pale white face, and black polish on her nails.

Mira grabbed a yellow plastic rake that usually resided in the sandbox and held it out defensively. "Who are you?"

"Don't be so jumpy," the girl said. "I'm not going to bite."

"I'm not jumpy," Mira said, though the hairs on the back of her neck stood on end. "Where'd you come from?" Her yard backed overgrown woods. She'd never seen a person in those woods, only animals.

The girl whistled, and the golden bird flew to light gently on her outstretched arm. His splendid coloring was even more startling up close. "I was just searching for Edwin here," the girl said. "Seeing where he'd gotten off to." She clucked at him affectionately.

The bird cooed at the girl, the crest laid back against his head.

"Oh. Is he your pet?" Mira said. "Did he get out of his cage?"

The girl didn't answer that. "I see you've held on to your nucleus of protection," she said. "Impressive."

The girl must be making fun of the plastic rake. Mira flung it down. "That's a toy. I don't know why I picked that up."

"I see," the girl said, in a way that meant she didn't.

The bird made a piercing chirrup.

"Be calm, Edwin," the girl said. "Yes, I see she wields protection against us. I had not expected it, but it does follow."

"I've put it down," Mira said. "I'm not holding it anymore."

"Have you, now? How long have you been here?" the girl said.

Mira felt her brow furrow. The conversation didn't feel quite right somehow. "I've always lived here. This is my house."

"With your parents, I presume?"

"No, they're in heaven." Mira did what she usually did when that question came up: held tight to her pendant and focused on taking in a breath. Then letting it out. A second breath in . . .

The girl's eyes went to Mira's fist on her pendant, and then she studied her face.

16

Mira studied the girl right back. The girl put Mira in mind of a mantis—with those wide-set amber eyes, small lips, and pointed chin—and that plum hair was an impossible shade.

"You and I should be friends," the girl said at last.

Mira didn't know what she'd expected the girl to say, but it certainly wasn't that. What an interesting proposition! The girl smelled like wilted flowers and . . . well, someone who hadn't bathed in a few days. Her white shirt and brown pants were stained and wrinkled. The black nail polish was chipped. She seemed to have come here directly from some exotic adventure. "Where do you live? How old are you? Do you go to the high school?" Mira said.

"My age is irrelevant, as my schooling is over. And where I live is . . . nearby."

"Where? On Nunnelly Farm Road?"

"Perhaps I will share that," the girl said, "if we decide to be friends."

Mira didn't have to think about it for long. Being friends with an older girl with an *I don't care* attitude might help Mira with the kids on the bus. It'd been hard to switch schools, to go to sixth grade at Loganville Middle. Mira didn't exactly have a lot of friendship offers on the table. "What's your name? Mine's Mira Blaise."

"Lyndame."

"Lyndame . . . what?"

"I don't use a surname."

"Okay, Lyndame, want to come in for breakfast?"

17

"Perhaps another time." Lyndame stepped forward. "Would you like to see my weapon?"

Mira took a step backward. "It isn't a gun, is it? I'm not allowed to look at guns."

"No, it is not." Lyndame took something from inside her left sleeve. A thin silver rod, the length of her forearm, cast in a way that made the metal look woven, with a sparkling stone ornament at the base. She held it out for inspection.

"A wand?" Mira said. She ought to have laughed. It wasn't as if a wand was an actual weapon. Or even an actual thing. But when Lyndame had taken out the wand, there was the faintest clang, like the striking of a bell in a distant land. The air turned still and cold. And Mira didn't feel like laughing.

"Is that a real diamond?" Mira said, and her face warmed. It couldn't be a real diamond. It was the size of a walnut.

Lyndame's serious tone matched hers. Even the golden bird wore a studious look, his eyes intent on the wand. "It is beautiful, isn't it?" Lyndame said. "Though the source of its power is very far away. It's not as powerful as it could be."

The sparkling of the wand was mesmerizing. "You mean . . . it doesn't do anything?"

"On the contrary," Lyndame said. "It can do a great deal."

"Like what?" Mira said.

Lyndame had long canine teeth; they gave her smile an aggressive quality. She leaned in to whisper, "For one, it can grant you wishes."

Chapter Four

Mira felt a surge of hope at the mention of wishes. Though she swallowed the hope down. Because really, all of that was impossible. "Wishes for *me*? What kind of wishes?"

"What would you wish for? What is it you want?" Lyndame tucked the wand back into her sleeve.

Mira spoke before she thought. "I wish life was like before Papa died. I wish he were still here."

From Lyndame's shoulder, Edwin made an alarmed chirrup.

"That is not an acceptable wish. It isn't possible to bring back the dead, not in any real sense." Lyndame studied her. "I think you know that."

Mira had suspected it. It was just the type of exception to wishes she'd read about in books. But she wasn't worried about it because she wasn't taking this conversation too seriously. She had the feeling this was some sort of game. That Lyndame was playing a part and so was Mira, though she wasn't sure what the parts were or even what the game was supposed to be. What *should* she wish for? The pile of laundry occurred to her, in the hall waiting for their Sunday afternoon washing. "Could I wish for a person to come and do jobs for me? Like, my chores when I ask them to?"

"Compulsion?" Lyndame said, frowning. "You didn't look like the sort of girl who would ask for that sort of thing."

Mira was regretting she'd not considered more carefully before speaking. Even if this was a game, it should be played correctly. And she didn't want Lyndame to get angry and leave. "Wait. I didn't mean to control someone. That came out wrong. Why don't you tell me what I *can* wish for?"

"The wand can bring you objects, items with physical form."

"Any object . . ." Mira considered. "What size do you mean? Like something really big? Or something really small?"

"Let us say an object of medium size," Lyndame said. "The wand's power is currently limited. I must conserve it. I can grant you three reasonably sized wishes, and no more."

More rules for Mira to think over.

"And afterward," Lyndame continued, "you might want to make me a gift in return. As one friend to another. That stone you wear, for instance."

Mira's hand went to her pendant. "No, not this. I couldn't give you this. Papa told me never to take it off. It was a gift from my mother." Mira wouldn't want to take it off in any case. She always felt better with it on. "But I could give you something else." Not that she had much. A book, maybe?

An unreadable expression passed over Lyndame's face. "It

doesn't matter. Perhaps I won't require anything of you. I feel for you. All lost and alone with no parents to defend you."

It was an odd statement. Mira didn't think on it until later, and by then she wasn't sure why it had seemed so odd. "So, you're saying I *wouldn't* have to pay?" That was good. She'd hate to part with any of her books.

"Yes, let's say that. I'll require nothing to grant wishes for a friend of mine."

"Mira!" It was Val, calling from the screened-in porch. She probably couldn't see Mira through the magnolia tree.

"I need to start making breakfast," Mira said.

"I'll depart," Lyndame said.

"Wait a minute. Don't go. I'll think of a wish." What kind of object would be best? A doe in the woods peered around a bush, as if she wanted to know too.

"No." Lyndame held up a palm. "Not so quickly, little Mira. You should consider carefully. Edwin and I will return at break of day tomorrow. You may give me your first wish then."

Mira was surprised to be called *little*. She was nearly as tall as Lyndame! But this game made Mira feel singled out, special in a way she hadn't felt since Papa had been gone. "All right," she said. "Thank you. Maybe afterward you could walk with me to the school bus? There are some kids that, uh, might want to meet you." Tomorrow was Monday, and she was thinking of Tisha and Jasmine. If those girls met Lyndame, they might stop pretending Mira didn't exist.

"Perhaps." Lyndame still wore a hint of that smile on her lips. "Just you think hard on your wish, little Mira."

Mira felt a thrill run through her. She *would* think hard on it. She definitely would.

Chapter Five

The four of them—Val, Sara, Beans, and Mira—were "belt tightening" according to Val, a process that'd been going on all year. It had nothing to do with belts. It had to do with spending less money. Val recently said they were "back on track," but each time Val brought up the belt tightening, Mira *did* feel like a belt was being pulled tight around her waist, pinching right in the pit of her stomach in what Gammy used to call Mira's "worry spot."

The public library was free. And as Mira had turned eleven in January, she was old enough to supervise the other girls at the library, so no need for a babysitter.

That was why on Sunday afternoon, they were again headed to the library. The girls would stay there and keep themselves occupied while Val worked with her friend Abbie cleaning a move-out.

In the back seat of Val's car, Mira was daydreaming about what she could wish for. A library for her bedroom? A trampoline? A Corvette? Or maybe those weren't reasonably sized wishes. She still wasn't sure what that meant. A diamond ring was small but expensive. A plastic wading pool was big, but she'd seen those on sale at Walmart for $19.97.

". . . and think about savings accounts for college now that the budget . . ." Val was talking. ". . . important because . . ." Something. Something. "Are you listening, Mira?"

Mira started. Val's blue eyes appeared briefly in the rearview mirror. Why was Val singling Mira out? A pain in her worry spot. "Yes, we need to save money for college," Mira said.

"You got it. Or secondary school of some kind. Your dad started a fund for you, and the survivor benefits will help, but you'll need more. My parents never saved a penny for me," Val said. "I don't want that for you all. In fact, did I tell you about that year when we had to eat out of the trash can at—"

"You told us!" Sara interrupted. "A million times. And there were flies. It was nasty."

"I don't wanna eat a fly!" Beans kicked at the front seats.

"That's not my point," Val said. "Oh, whatever. Here we are."

They were pulling up to the curb in front of the library.

Mira hopped out of the car, and her eye was caught by a flash of gold in the cherry tree by the doors. She squinted. Yes, it was the bird, Edwin, perched near the top of the tree. The bird was like a little sun up there, radiant and beautiful.

Mira felt dull by comparison. She wore weekend clothes: a brick-colored T-shirt that was much too big—it read *Northwest Exterminating*, Papa's former company; indigo pants that were much too short; and of course, her trusty purple flip-flops—she

24

wore Band-Aids where they'd rubbed blisters on her toes.

Val leaned out the car window. "Now remember, no talking to strangers. If a person approaches you, you march directly to the front desk. Scream if you have to. You hear me?"

The girls mumbled their agreement. It was nothing they hadn't heard before.

"I want to play with the dollhouse," Beans said.

That wasn't surprising. The dollhouse—actually called the Waystation—was the most popular attraction in the children's room. It was a castle-like building full of nooks and crannies, ladders and stairs extending to strange rooms, and was populated by figures of all sizes and shapes, including ogres, fairies, and creatures Mira didn't have a name for, many of which carried suitcases (which really opened!) and various odd parcels. There was even a painted lake that contained, of all things, red plastic squid. *Where will your imagination take you?* the sign said.

Mira stole one last look at the golden bird in the tree. It was like he was following her, spying on her. The thought made her walk through the doors a little faster.

They all said hello to the ferret sleeping in his penthouse, and then Beans whispered loudly, "Dolls!"

"No playing until you say hello to Miss Liu," Mira said.

Beans sighed heavily and trudged over to the librarian's desk. "Hello, Miss Liu," she said in a robotic voice.

The frames of Miss Liu's glasses matched her smooth black hair. A sideways smile was on her heart-shaped face. "The book you wanted is in."

25

Beans sucked in a breath. "The one with the princess?"

"That's the one. I see you dressed for it. It's on the reserved shelf. No running—"

Beans was already running off, tripping over her princess dress as she went.

Miss Liu clucked and shook her head, but she still wore the smile.

"Sorry," Mira said to Miss Liu. "I'll remind her."

Miss Liu was clicking on her computer keyboard. "You girls have fun today, but remember . . ." She pointed to a sign: *Be Mindful of Others!*

"Yes, Miss Liu," Mira said.

Mira wanted to say more. She wanted to ask for Miss Liu's advice. Miss Liu was nice and always had good advice. But Mrs. Bongle was close by, sorting through books on a cart. Mrs. Bongle was not so nice, and her advice usually ran along the lines of *Keep it down!* or *Do you want me to call your parents?* Mira would have to wait.

In the children's room, Beans was in a beanbag chair reading her princess book, so Mira settled into a chair to read.

"Want to play checkers?" Sara said. Her blond hair was shorter than ever, Mira noted; she must've gotten into the shears again.

A brief image of them playing checkers, cheating each other and laughing like ordinary sisters, passed through Mira's mind. But then she pictured how they would look sitting at the checkerboard table: petite Sara and big, gangly Mira. It reminded her how out of place she was, how she didn't really fit. "I'm reading right now."

Sara glanced down at Mira's empty hands, and her cheeks turned red and she went off toward the Legos.

"I meant I'm getting ready to read. I'm getting my book out now!" Mira called after her. The chair suddenly felt uncomfortable, so she moved to sit on the carpet with her back against a bookshelf.

After two chapters, a familiar noise cut into the story. Beans, bouncing around, pretending to be a rabbit. If Beans wasn't under control, Mrs. Bongle would call Val at work and then Val would be upset with them. Mira could not afford for that to happen. She put down her book to color with Beans, read books aloud, and play at the Waystation.

Finally, at about four in the afternoon, while Mira was reading yet another book to Beans in the beanbag chair, the younger girl's eyes fluttered. Beans clutched at Mira with a sweaty little hand. "Stay with me, Mira." *Miwa.* A second later, Beans was breathing deeply, sound asleep.

Mira sighed in relief and gently inched her hand out from under the younger girl's. She asked Sara to watch Beans for a minute, then headed out of the children's room, in search of Miss Liu.

Near the front desk, Mira ran into Shanice and her friend Chloe. Chloe stood next to Shanice in what used to be Mira's spot. The girls wore warm-up pants over gymnastics clothes, fancy makeup, their hair in tight buns with traces of glitter. They must've come straight from a meet.

"Mira!" Shanice said. "Nice to see you."

"Geez. You look like you just got out of bed," Chloe said.

Mira was suddenly very aware of the fact that she *had* slept in Papa's old T-shirt and she hadn't combed her hair all day.

"Who cares? It's Sunday," Shanice said. And she smiled at Mira, displaying that familiar gap between her front teeth.

Mira returned the smile gratefully. In Mira's life *before*, she and Shanice had been inseparable. They met when they were six, in the first day of gymnastics clinics, and realized they both went to Western Prince Academy, shared a favorite color (yellow), and could each do a dead-on imitation of Grover from *Sesame Street*. Since then, Mira had stayed over at Shanice's house so often, Shanice's mother bought a sleeping bag for Mira to keep in Shanice's room. Mira felt a twinge in her stomach. She wondered if the sleeping bag was now being used by Chloe.

"It's good to see you. We've missed you," Shanice said.

"Are you guys looking for a book?" Mira said, and then inwardly cringed. Of course they were looking for a book! This was the library!

Chloe snorted, but Shanice merely said, "Yeah, I still can't figure out what to do my social studies essay on."

"Not like it's due tomorrow or anything," Chloe said.

Mira didn't understand why Shanice liked Chloe. The girl seemed to spend all her time fiddling with her long highlights and looking for ways to be snarky. She'd been in gymnastics with them since the beginning, but Mira and Shanice had never paid much attention to her.

"Text sometime, okay? We can get together," Shanice said.

"I don't have a phone. Mine . . . broke," Mira said. A lie. Mira's phone had been a "belt tightening" casualty. Why was Mira lying to Shanice? Maybe it was because Chloe was standing where Mira used to stand, and everybody knew Chloe's family had four cars and an entertainment room.

"I hope you get another one soon," Shanice said. "At least before camp starts."

"Me too," Mira said, and that was a second lie. Because she wasn't going to be at camp. Val had already told her that she wouldn't be able to swing the monthlong gymnastics camp this summer.

"Oh, there's Mom texting me," Shanice said. "Let me go grab a book. Let's meet at the pool as soon as school's out. 'Kay?"

"Okay," Mira said. And that was number three. Val said they couldn't be members of the pool this summer because Mrs. Sutter wasn't able to drive them there and Val was going to be too tired when she got home.

Mira would probably never see Shanice again as long as she lived.

Chapter Six

Miss Liu walked by, carrying a cardboard box. "Are you okay, Mira?"

"Yes," Mira said, although she hadn't moved from the spot near the library's front desk where she'd bumped into Shanice and Chloe. Her eyes felt itchy.

Miss Liu gave her a long look. "Would you like to assist me in the common room? I'm setting up for book club."

Mira nodded and followed her. When they got to the door of the common room, Mira paused. The room was full of desks and chairs. "Are you sure it's okay for me to be in here?"

"This is a public room. And the club meeting doesn't start for a half hour." Miss Liu took a notebook from her box and put it at one of the desks. "Would you get the pencils out of that cabinet? You can put one at each spot."

Mira located the box of pencils and put one out. Then another. They'd gotten halfway around the room when Mira remembered what she wanted to talk to Miss Liu about. "So," Mira said in an offhand way, "what if someone said they could grant you wishes? Would you wish for something?"

Miss Liu looked startled. "Why do you ask? Are you reading a book about wishes? Writing a story?"

"I might. For now, I'm just thinking about it. So . . . what do you think?"

"You're talking about wishing to live forever, that type of thing?"

"No thanks. I've read *Tuck Everlasting*."

"Have the love of your life sweep you off your feet?" The sideways smile was back.

"Ewww, no. I'm being serious. If someone said you could have wishes, would you believe it?"

"I believe many things are possible, so yes, I might believe it."

"What would you wish for?" Mira said.

"I'm not sure. How many wishes would I get?"

"Three."

"Right, of course. It's always three, isn't it? I don't know. Wishes are dangerous. You know how it goes . . . You wish to go back in time to make your life better, but then you accidentally change something so that someone you loved never existed or you erase your own existence."

Worry pooled in Mira's stomach. "That, um, happens?"

"Well, in *books*, of course, like we're talking about." Miss Liu had gotten ahead of Mira. She gestured for Mira to keep going with the box of pencils.

"What if the wish had to be for an object?"

"Ah, that *is* limiting. Would this person want something in return?"

"What if they were only being nice? Like, they wanted to be friends with you."

"Then I might ask for something. I'm not sure." Miss Liu took a pack of water bottles from the cabinet and absently began placing one at each desk.

"What kind of things?"

"If I *did* want to make a wish, and I'm not saying I would because you haven't given me enough information, I'd start with something small, something I really needed. And I'd word the wish carefully. Wish grantors are usually tricksters trying to hurt you. Like you wish for gold, and a box of bullion falls from the sky and crushes you. Or you wish for wings to fly, and then you're *only* able to fly and not walk anymore. Or you wish for a ring to turn you invisible, but you don't specify one that can turn you *visible* again, and then, you know."

Wow. Miss Liu certainly had a wild imagination. "Okay . . ." Mira said. "I guess I'd need to be careful with the wording. I only know that whatever I wish for has to be, like, a thing, and it can't be too big or too small."

Miss Liu's smooth brow wrinkled. "This is all hypothetical, isn't it? Pretend? You'd know better than to take a wish from a stranger, wouldn't you?"

It was *probably* pretend, so Mira wasn't lying, not really. "I'm just thinking of a strategy in case someone *did* offer me wishes." She took her time positioning a pencil.

A pause. "Well, okay, then . . . I'd also be sure of the price. A trickster might act like the price isn't much, but I've never heard of magic with no price."

Mira's head spun. Miss Liu sure had plenty of thoughts on the matter.

"*Miss* Liu," came a sharp voice. It was Mrs. Bongle at the doorway, her hands on her hips.

Miss Liu flinched and nearly dropped a water bottle. "I thought you were on an errand."

"No children in here except during children's programming hours," Mrs. Bongle said.

"I didn't know," Miss Liu said.

"It's *in* the handbook, page seventeen, section three," Mrs. Bongle said. "I see this one around here quite often. Where are her parents?"

"She's old enough to be here by herself," Miss Liu said. And to Mira, "Go back to the children's room, all right?"

Mrs. Bongle harrumphed, eyes on Mira as she hurried out.

"I'm sorry," Miss Liu was saying again.

Mira felt bad Miss Liu was in trouble, but Mira wasn't sorry they'd had the conversation. It had been very interesting. She would need to be much more careful than she'd thought.

I'd start with something small.

Chapter Seven

After dinner Sunday night, Mira put the dishes in the dishwasher, then headed for the stairs to the attic.

Val popped out of the bathroom, where she'd been helping Beans get ready for her bath. "Mira, wait. I wanted to thank you for cooking a great dinner."

"Mm-hmm," Mira said. Country fried steak and rice. They always had that on Sunday nights after chores.

"Hey, we're the same height now," Val said. "Did you notice?"

Mira glanced at her and was surprised to be looking right into Val's blue eyes. She quickly looked away again. "You're the same height as someone who's eleven? Maybe you should work on that. Do some stretches."

"Ha ha. Very funny," Val said, though Mira had actually been serious. "How was school this week? You haven't really said."

"Good." It hadn't been. It never was. But there was no point in mentioning it.

"Momma!" Beans called from the bathroom.

"Just a minute, honey," Val said. And to Mira, "Would you

want to spend some time downstairs with us tonight? We could make some popcorn."

"Is Beans going to watch that kid show?" Mira said. Lately, Beans was obsessed with *Dinosaur Train*. She would watch episode after episode after episode.

"Well, yes, it's an appropriate one for her age. But after she goes to bed, we can watch a show you like. You've been spending a lot of time in your room, don't you think?"

Mira shrugged.

"And . . . I was wondering if we could talk about some things, like how you like living here with us." Val's voice had taken on an overly-casual-somehow-fake tone.

The tone put Mira on edge. Maybe because Mira didn't *want* to talk about how she liked living there. She had figured out the balance in the house: she did her chores and helped with the meals and went to school and did her homework and everything seemed to hang together, it seemed to work. She didn't want things to change. "It's fine. It's all good. Really."

"I know this year has been hard for you. It's been hard on all of us . . ." Val blinked, then blinked again.

Oh no. Was Val going to cry? Was she going to cry about Papa? Or was she going to talk about the other horrible occurrence from that terrible day—the thing Val had done? At the thought, the heat, the anger rushed into Mira's chest, traveling all the way to her cheeks. Val had apologized profusely, but they hadn't talked about it since and Mira did *not* want to. "Can I go now?" Mira said. "I'm really sleepy."

"The tub is running over!" Beans yelled.

"Beans!" Val said. "How many times have I told you to wait for me to turn on . . ." And she was dashing to the bathroom, and Mira escaped quickly up the stairs.

✳ ✳ ✳

A short time later, Mira sat cross-legged on her bed while raindrops beat on the attic roof.

Mira's mother had liked the sound of rain. Papa had told Mira that. Also, a cozy fire, planting flowers, and working in the garden. Mira didn't know much more. What was her mother's favorite cereal? Her favorite color? Her favorite animal? Papa hadn't been sure. He hadn't known if she'd had any family either, sisters or brothers, nothing. He said Mira's mother hadn't liked talking about herself but that he *knew enough*. Mira had no memories of her own—she'd been only three months old when her mother died.

Mira flopped onto her stomach and held on to her pendant while she stroked an ivory silk square in the quilt. Gammy had made the quilt for Mira, piecing it together with velvet from one of her old dresses, plaid from Papa's discarded shirts, and that ivory silk from Mira's mother's wedding gown. *Your mother loved you and your Papa very much*, Gammy said. *We'll weave that love into your quilt.* The square of silk didn't feel like love—what was that supposed to feel like?—but it did feel soft.

A glance at the framed photograph on the bureau. Beneath

that billowy veil, Mira's mother had been a fair, slight woman with brown hair, wide-set eyes, a pinched nose, and a timid smile. Mira didn't resemble her mother—even she could see that; with Mira's long-legged, bony body, tan skin with a tendency to freckle, rounded olive-green eyes, and "strong" nose (a description Mira didn't particularly enjoy), she looked more like Papa. Mira's mother hadn't liked having her picture taken, according to Papa, didn't like to be the center of attention, didn't like to make a fuss. The wedding photo was the only one Mira had.

Her mother was wearing the pendant in the photograph. Mira clutched the stone tighter. She wanted to keep the memory of her mother close to her heart, but she didn't have much to put there.

A tapping at the window. A small black shape, hunched over, feathers soaked. Bandit, tapping with his bill.

"Really?" Mira said. "You're out in the rain?"

She got up from the bed and opened the window. He side-step-hopped onto a stack of storage containers.

"What are you doing out in this?" Mira said.

He gave a soft caw, stretched out his wings, and shook water all over.

She wiped raindrops from her cheeks. "Well, that's a mess. But I'm glad you're here. You can give me some advice."

He looked at her sideways out of a beady brown eye. That was his normal way of looking at her, so it probably didn't mean more than *Do you have my treats?*

She took a small handful of unsalted peanuts from the jar

she kept near the window and put them on the lid of the storage container. He gulped each nut whole.

"Do you think magical wishes could be real?" she asked him.

He eyed her.

"I think it's possible too," Mira said. "That means I should definitely make a wish, just in case. A *smart* wish."

He eyed the spot where the peanuts had been.

She put out a few more. "I agree. I shouldn't wish for something too big, because of what Miss Liu said. It could be a trap."

He gobbled the peanuts. He was such a glutton.

"So, I think I should wish for—"

The crow made a great swoop for the bureau. He knocked over the wedding photo of Mira's parents, toppled a stack of books, and quickly made out the window with one of her pencils.

"I'm trying to have a serious discussion here!" Mira shouted after him. "Pencils don't grow on trees, you know!"

She slammed the window closed. She should have expected it. That was the third pencil he'd taken in a week. And he'd left a poop for her on top of the storage container. "Gee, thanks, Bandit," she said.

He hadn't even stayed to hear what she was going to wish for.

Her gaze fell on her flip-flops, discarded at the top of the staircase. The stairs were there because her attic room wasn't really a bedroom. It was a loft storage space filled with extra furniture and boxes.

Some kids wore flip-flops to school—sure they did. But it made recess awkward. It was impossible to run in them, so she had to wear smelly and ill-fitting shoes from Coach Josh's extra athletic shoes bin. Plus, it'd be nice to have real shoes without having to ask Val for them.

And maybe . . . new shoes could be the start of a change for Mira. When Val had said they didn't have the tuition money for her private school, Mira started at the public school, Loganville Middle. The kids were nice enough, but Mira was so sad about Papa, she didn't make an effort to get to know any of them, ghosting through the days, mostly eating her lunch in the school counselor's office. Soon the kids seemed to think of her as a ghost; she got put into the category of *quiet girl who nobody pays attention to* and wasn't sure how to get out of it. Lately, this kid Dublin had sort of adopted her, showing up next to her at random moments, but he was pretty busy with Math Club.

Maybe now was the time to make an effort, really try to fit in. If the wish worked, if she actually got new shoes, maybe it would be a sign. A sign that it was time for a change. New shoes could represent a step, so to speak, in the right direction.

She tried not to get her hopes up too much. The whole wish business was probably just pretend. She felt a smile twitching at her lips. Because what if it wasn't?

It was hard to fall asleep that night. She was too excited.

Chapter Eight

Mira rarely closed the blinds in the attic, because of Bandit's unscheduled visits, so she woke with the sun most days. The next morning, at the first sign of light, she threw back her quilt and hopped out of bed, dashing down the stairs.

Outside, it was colder than usual and she shivered in her shorts and T-shirt, her bare feet wet from the dew. Plenty of birds were up and about, chirping away, but there was no sign of the golden bird.

"Hello?" Mira said, peering up into the branches of the magnolia.

"What are you doing?" Picking her way through the yard, Sara was already dressed for school: a unicorn T-shirt, a silver barrette in her short blond hair.

Good grief. It was so hard to get away from them.

"Just leave me alone, okay?" Mira said.

"I want to see the animals too."

"If you go inside, I'll let you touch my necklace." That bribe usually worked. Sara was jealous of her necklace, Mira knew.

The only memento Sara had from her biological father was a plastic hairbrush; the man had apparently vanished from their lives, leaving only that.

"I'm staying out," Sara said. "You can't make me go in. You're not the boss of me."

"I'll do your sweeping." Sweeping was Sara's Monday chore.

"I don't mind sweeping." That was probably true. Sara would ride the broom around pretending to be a witch as she swept. "Mira, do you think pixies are real?" Sara added.

"What?" Mira followed Sara's gaze. Fairy Village *did* always look magical in the mornings. It gave Mira a strange half-remembered feeling. A feeling from when she was little. She had definitely believed in pixies back then. Mira suddenly remembered something else. Something Papa had said: he'd built the village based on a request from Mira's mother because making pixies feel welcome supposedly brought good luck. Maybe Mira's mother had believed in them. "Why are you talking about pixies?"

"Never mind. I'm joking," Sara said.

Mira didn't understand the joke. But she didn't have time to ask more questions. She needed to get Sara back inside, no matter the cost. "What if I play a board game with you?" Mira said. "After school. I'll do it if you go inside right this minute."

Sara narrowed her eyes. "Fox in the Forest. And it has to be after school *today*. Three full games. We wear the game hats and make popcorn on the stove."

"Two games. Popcorn but no hats." The hats had been an

41

invention of Papa's, and using them these days made Mira feel sad.

"Deal." Sara hop-skipped toward the house.

"I pity the child who wants affection from you," Lyndame said. From her shoulder, Edwin added a chirp like an exclamation point. They were in the woods, hanging back in the shadows.

"She doesn't need affection from me," Mira said. "She has a mother for that."

"Ah," Lyndame said. "Back to the wishing, then. Remember, no compulsion. And no attempting to bring people back from the dead either."

"I know that. And see here, for my first wish, I'm going to ask for something small that I really need." Mira added a big smile. It probably made her look like that suck-up Kay Anders, who was always smiling at the math teacher, hoping for extra credit. But if Lyndame saw that Mira wasn't greedy, maybe Lyndame wouldn't turn the wished-for objects into deadly projectiles.

"And what, pray tell, is that?"

"Shoes like the other kids have. Not permanently attached or too, um, heavy. Just regular shoes. Maybe even some that are in style . . . if you want."

Lyndame stepped out from the shadows, and the sunlight fell onto the plum braid, the purple lipstick, the heavy black eyeliner. On her shoulder, Edwin was beautifully gold in the sunlight. He adjusted his feathers as if he knew it. "That's your first wish, then?" Lyndame said. "You're sure? You have only three." She was more eager than Mira would have expected.

"Um, yes." Mira pretended that her head itched, but she was really putting her hand up for protection, in case something fell on her, something like a heavy pair of shoes in a department store shopping bag.

Lyndame took the wand from her sleeve with a flash of silver light. The chirping of the birds instantly quieted, the wind died, and Mira could hear the sound of her own breathing.

A swirl of the wand as if Lyndame was signing her name on the air. "Enrobe," she said.

In front of them, the word *appeared*, hanging in the air by itself, written in shining sparks of light. Then the word broke apart and the sparks fell to cover an astonished Mira, tingling her bare arms and prickling her scalp. Mira held her breath as the sparks grew brighter and brighter until there was a *pop* and Mira had to close her eyes.

When she opened them again, she wore shoes, to be sure. What shoes! Dazzlingly white sneakers with gold laces and stars on the sides and soles so soft it was as if she floated on air. No more blisters. No more Band-Aids. She loved them instantly. The shoes looked familiar. "Wait, are these . . . ?" She couldn't think of the name, but she knew the brand was really expensive.

"Yes," Lyndame said. "They are."

And Lyndame hadn't stopped at the shoes. Mira wore stylish jeans, a T-shirt that read *Killing It*, and a white cardigan with black stripes; an animal-print backpack was slung on her shoulder. There was a lovely smell in the air like pumpkin spice, and Mira's hair felt different, swishier. She let it fall over a cheek. "Is my hair . . . curled?"

"Never let it be said that Lyndame doesn't know how to fulfill a wish. This should help with your little problems on the coach."

"You mean the school bus?" Mira said. Lyndame had spoken truth. This actually might help. "You did all this with one word?"

Lyndame sniffed. "The words don't matter so much; they're just a way to focus the magic. *I* could do it without them. It's all in the visualization."

It was certainly more than Mira could have visualized, or even thought possible. The backyard seemed to be covered in a haze of joy. "This is great! Thank you so much!" She tried to hug Lyndame, but the girl recoiled.

"I don't hug," Lyndame said. "Let us just take our cordial leave. Until tomorrow, then. At dawn, we'll be here for your second wish. Meanwhile, enjoy the first one."

She and Edwin melted back into the woods while Mira did cartwheels in the yard.

Chapter Nine

Mira stood tall at the bus stop, still feeling some of the fizzy joy from earlier.

Her head spun with unanswered questions—*why* had Lyndame appeared and *how* did the magic work and *where* did Lyndame come from—but those questions were so big and overwhelming that they went slip-sliding around in Mira's mind, never settling in one spot for her to focus on, particularly in light of the glowing realization that she looked *really, really good*. Better than she'd ever looked, actually, even when Papa and Gammy were still here.

She put down her brand-spanking-new backpack and did another cartwheel just for fun, although the pavement was rough on her palms, and when she popped up, a sparrow landed on her shoulder and nuzzled at her ear.

"Tralalalala!" Mira sang to it.

The sparrow, startled, flew off, and Mira laughed, calling after it, "Sorry!"

Tisha and Jasmine walked up shortly after, talking and

laughing. They lived next door to each other and always came together to the bus stop. They didn't speak to Mira. They never spoke to Mira.

But today was different. Mira looked just like Tisha and Jasmine. She was one of them, she thought—she fit right in. So today, instead of taking out her book and keeping her head down, Mira said, "Hey."

Tisha's eyes widened, but she responded, "Hey," and her gaze traveled all the way down to Mira's shoes, taking in Mira's new look. Tisha whispered something to Jasmine, and then they giggled behind their hands. When they'd done that on previous days, Mira had ignored them. But today, the day she was equal to them in every way, she said, "What's so funny?"

"It's just . . . it's so cute, how you're dressed," Tisha said. The words should have been flattering, but they weren't. She appeared to be trying hard not to laugh.

Jasmine seemed to want to fix the situation. "No, really. Those are great knockoffs. Where'd you get them?"

Mira looked down at her shoes. The girls thought they were imitations of the brand. They didn't think they were *real.* "They're not knockoffs."

"If you say so." Tisha erupted into a fit of giggles. "It's really nice you washed your hair, though, I've got to say."

It probably wouldn't help matters to explain that they only had one bathroom and it was hard to get much time in there. Mira said nothing.

"Let's check out *your* hair, to see if you washed," Jasmine said, messing up Tisha's hair and generally trying to be a distraction—at least it seemed that way. Jasmine was definitely the nicer of the two.

Yet by the time the bus arrived, the girls were giggling behind their hands again.

At that moment, Mira knew just how the rest of the day was going to go. And by the end of the day, she was proven right.

All day long, the kids whispered. When she tried to locate the source, the whispering stopped. It didn't take long before she wished she was wearing something else. Anything else. The glorious clothes seemed to have created a target on her back. Being invisible had been far preferable. Dublin clued her in over plates of grilled cheese at lunch: the kids were saying she was a shoplifter. All the rest of the day, as she walked the halls, the other kids seemed to move away from her. She was a floating island of aloneness.

Getting on the school bus to go home, Tisha wasn't even pretending to be nice. "I'm going to talk to my mom about you," she said, her voice stern, and turned without another word to climb the stairs onto the bus.

Jasmine smiled sadly and shrugged. She followed Tisha up the bus steps.

Mira remembered then: Tisha's mom owned Shampooch Palace, where Val worked.

The afternoon at home was not going to go well, Mira thought.

She was right about that too.

* * *

A few hours later, Val was saying, "I'm going to ask you one more time. Where'd you get them?" She sat across the kitchen table from Mira. The handyman, James, had just left, having added yet more locks to the house, this time to the bathroom window.

"I told you, I wished for them," Mira said.

"From who?"

Mira couldn't tell Val about Lyndame; she just couldn't. Now that Mira knew the wishes really worked, she needed her last two wishes to be good ones. "It was . . . nobody."

"Did you steal them?"

"I already told you I didn't."

Val rubbed her face. "I don't understand this. I just asked Morgan for a raise, told her what a difficult year it's been. And now she's calling me with concerns her daughter has. I wondered why you went out to the bus stop so early this morning. You didn't want me to notice the clothes, did you? I just want to be able to explain this. You've put me in an awkward position here."

"Me?" Mira said. "How did I do that?" *She* was the one who felt awkward, having to ask Val for clothes, for shoes, for everything.

"I need to know who gave them to you. Was it someone you met online? I've *told* you girls to be careful online."

"No," Mira said.

"I just don't understand why you're acting out like this."

Getting new clothes was acting out? All the events of the day,

48

all that miserable aloneness, roiled in Mira's stomach. "Whatever." She crossed her arms and blinked fiercely. She would not cry. She would not.

"Has something happened to upset you? Do you want to talk about it?"

It seemed to come up out of the wretchedness in her stomach. "I hate my school!" Mira blurted. "I want to go back to Western Prince. I need to go back to Western Prince. All my friends are there." She hadn't planned on saying that. She hadn't begged for anything this year. Not once.

"Western Prince? Not likely. Not unless you were to suddenly get some great scholarship that came with transportation. It's a private school. Your dad had to really stretch . . . You realize that, don't you? Western Prince." Val was chuckling.

Mira felt her cheeks flame. Of course she knew that. She knew about the belt tightening. She knew why she had to switch schools. Logically, she knew. She just missed her friends.

"You're going to need to spend some time in your room," Val said. "And we'll need to talk more about this later. I hope this doesn't mean my job."

"I have to start the quesadillas," Mira said. She always made quesadillas on Mondays. Always.

"Not tonight," Val said.

"Then you'll have to make them yourself," Mira said.

Val's smile was ghoulish. "I suppose I can manage. Go on up. And leave those clothes on the stairs. Those shoes, especially. You can't wear them anymore."

Mira's eyes filled with tears. Not only had the clothes not worked like she'd hoped, but Val was being really mean. All Val cared about was saving money and her own daughters and keeping the house locked up tight like a vault.

She's awful, Mira thought as she stomped up the stairs. *She hates me.* Mira knew it was true because of the thing Val had done, the thing Mira could never forgive, the horrible thing on that terrible day. Mira blinked back her tears. She could not forget.

* * *

That evening, Mira was in her attic bedroom, stretching on the tumbling mat she used for a carpet. She hadn't gone downstairs for dinner because she wasn't hungry.

Although Mira tried to shut it out, Mrs. Sutter's voice played in her head: *You should be thankful, girl, that your father had the foresight to get married and make sure you were taken care of. Got Val roped in, just in the nick of time, didn't he? Got her good and stuck with you.*

As if Papa could have known what would happen, only weeks after he married Val . . .

A sharp pain in her chest. Mira didn't want to think about that anymore.

Sara and Beans were coming. They clambered up the stairs, dragging an object behind them that made a *thump* against each step.

When Val and the girls had moved into the house, Mira

asked Papa to move her stuff up to the attic rather than share a room with Sara. Sara and Beans had come up so often since then, though, that the attic hadn't really given Mira the privacy she'd hoped for.

"Can we come in?" Sara said, peering through the balusters and between the boxes that Mira had tried to make into a wall to keep them out.

Mira sighed. "Yeah. I'm sorry I forgot about the board games. We can play now. I can't make popcorn, though. I'm not allowed to leave my room."

Beans tripped on the last stair. A Candy Land game smacked the floor, and she landed atop the box with a grunt.

Sara slid past Beans. She presented Mira with microwave pizza rolls in a napkin. "I made them myself." The napkin was soggy, but the rolls were hot and smelled pretty good.

Beans dragged the game over and heaved it onto the mat. "'S your favorite!" she said.

Mira was pretty sure Candy Land was *Beans's* favorite, not hers. "Thought you wanted Fox in the Forest. Thought you said this game was boring," she said to Sara.

Sara shrugged.

Mira pulled her legs in close, resting her chin on her knees, while she waited for the pizza rolls to cool and for Beans to set up the board the way she liked (facing her, unsurprisingly).

"You can be blue," Sara announced, handing out the mover pieces. She usually demanded the blue piece for herself. It was a concession.

"No, it's okay. I'll be red," Mira said.

"I'll be Cutie-Pie," Beans said. Cutie-Pie was a doll-sized piece of pie they used in place of the lost yellow piece.

Mira and Sara exchanged glances and they snickered. Beans was *always* Cutie-Pie.

"You first," Beans said, pushing the spinner wheel toward Mira.

Maybe tomorrow would be better than today, Mira thought, spinning the arrow to see what her move would be. That's right— tomorrow she could make another wish. And she would come up with something better to wish for. Something that would let her move forward.

Something that would make everything just perfect.

Chapter Ten

Mira dreamed of a piece of paper Shanice had once shown her: a letter with the Western Prince Academy crest at the top. The letter described a merit scholarship award for the upcoming year. Shanice had been so pleased with herself.

When Mira opened her eyes in the morning, she leaped out of bed.

"A letter is an object," Mira said to the three mice gazing into the window. "Oh yeah, it is." She slid up the sash and put out the popcorn pieces she'd been saving for them. "Don't let Val see you, Moc, Croc, and Toc. Time for the dance party!"

Mira danced around. Her hair was getting in her eyes, so she rummaged for a hair tie and then walked on her hands for the mice. She walked the length of the room, then dropped to her feet and danced some more. The mice kept watching, cheeks full, paws on the windowpane.

This was the right sort of wish. Mira had always fit in at Western Prince. It was a place she truly belonged.

Not many minutes later, Mira was out in the backyard near

the ash tree, reading her own letter from Western Prince, courtesy of Lyndame.

"Starting today?" Mira glanced down at the new outfit she wore: a denim miniskirt, a colorful polka-dot shirt, high-top sneakers in a glittery silver. Mira looked so put together, so stylish, although again she'd not asked Lyndame for the clothes, just for the scholarship letter for school. Lyndame sure did go all out on wish fulfillment.

Mira felt like she might burst from excitement.

"I believe the bus will be arriving soon," Lyndame said.

"The minibus?" When Mira had attended Western Prince, she rode the minibus to school in the mornings. After school, she had taken the activities bus to the gymnastics center.

At Lyndame's nod, Mira thanked her, then celebrated with an energetic roundoff to a backflip. She faked crowd cheering noises as a trio of chickadees buzzed around her.

Bandit flew by carrying a celebratory pink-flamingo swizzle stick he'd probably shamelessly stolen right out of someone's drink.

Mira laughed as she dashed up the back steps to the screened-in porch and into the house. "Look at this!" she cried, rushing into the kitchen with the letter.

Val was pouring coffee, already wearing her Shampooch Palace T-shirt, though her hair was still wet from the shower. She blinked several times as she read. "This letter is dated today and the scholarship starts today? Where'd this come from?"

"Special delivery," Mira said.

"You mean it came by courier?" Val said.

"That's right," Mira said. "A courier."

"It's odd I didn't hear the doorbell," Val said.

"I want French toast," Beans interrupted. She sat at the table.

"Not today," Mira said. "The WP bus is coming soon. *That* stands for Western Prince. I've got to go."

"You're going back to your old school?" Sara said.

"Yes!" Mira said.

"But I want French toast," Beans said. "It's time for French toast."

"It's just so strange," Val said, studying the letter. "Scholarships usually start at the beginning of the school year, not near the end. Did you apply for this? I didn't even know they had these."

"I did," Mira said. "I did apply for it." Maybe not how Val meant, but Mira did make an application, in a way.

"Well, I'm happy for you," Val said, finally folding the letter, though she still looked confused. "It's what you wanted. Transportation too." Her gaze focused on Mira's clothes. "Wait. What are you—"

"Here's the bus!" Mira said, spying it out the window, pulling up directly in front of their driveway. No more walking up the street and dealing with Tisha and Jasmine. Mira ran out of the house without worrying about a backpack, a lunch, or even a pencil.

But there was Val, huffing up the driveway behind her. "Where did you get those clothes? You cannot accept clothes from strangers. I told you that. I will *not* allow it."

"It wasn't a stranger," Mira said. "It was a friend. A friend who felt sorry for me!" She hadn't meant to say it, didn't realize she was thinking it and definitely hadn't meant to shout it. "Um . . ."

Val's face looked stricken. "I didn't think . . . We just got you some new . . ."

The bus door squealed open. The driver was a gray-haired woman with sparkling eyes. "Good morning," she said to the two of them.

Mira was happy to see her former bus driver and also happy to change the subject. "Hello, Mrs. Jackson!"

"This bus goes to Western Prince?" Val asked. Which was a silly question, Mira thought. The name of the school was written in large letters on the side of the bus.

"Yes, ma'am," Mrs. Jackson said. "Mira's my first pickup of the day. Got the call this morning to add her to the route. Returning student, they said."

Val's face was scrunched. "They let you know this morning? Isn't that late notice?"

"I suppose," Mrs. Jackson said. "But they do what they want, that school. I just follow instructions."

Val still looked confused.

Mira bounced up the steps onto the bus. "It's all good. I'll see you later!" she called out to Val.

"What about after school?" Val said to the driver. "She gets a ride home too?"

"Righto," Mrs. Jackson said. "I'll get her home safe and sound. 'Bout three fifteen."

"We'll talk about those clothes tonight!" Val called to Mira.

Mira waved to her, then chose a seat halfway back. The seats were more comfortable than the public school's bus. Also, there was no chewing gum stuck beneath the seats or curse words carved into the vinyl with pen. The seats even had seat belts. She sighed in contentment.

Val finally gave up and Mrs. Jackson was able to drive away.

"Welcome back, my dear," the driver called out to Mira.

Mira beamed at her.

After a few minutes, Mrs. Jackson picked up a boy Mira recognized, though she couldn't remember his name. Mira waved at him, and he looked surprised but returned the wave before he slid into a seat near the front.

Mrs. Jackson picked up a girl that Mira didn't know. Mira waved at her too.

The next stop was a fawn-colored house with light blue shingles that Mira knew at once.

Shanice squealed when she got onto the bus. "Mira-boo!" She slid in next to Mira with her gap-toothed smile bigger than ever and insisted on explanations immediately. How was Mira back? How had this happened?

Mira told her about the scholarship. She might have left out a few parts. Mainly about Lyndame and the wishes.

"This is so awesome. I'm so glad you're back. Good old normal Mira." Shanice gave Mira's shoulders a squeeze.

Normal, Mira thought. It didn't seem like a huge compliment, but she was so happy to be back, to feel like she was in a place she belonged, she didn't worry about it. Or the fact that she'd taken anything *but* a normal route to get back.

"Chloe-Coe!" Shanice said when the girl boarded the bus. Chloe's face fell when she saw Mira.

Uh-oh, Mira thought. She would have assumed Chloe's parents would be driving her to school in one of their many cars.

"Sit here, my dear," Shanice said, her voice extra cheery, and Chloe obediently sat in front of them. No doubt she usually sat next to Shanice.

"I like your shirt," Mira said to Chloe, feeling generous. Then she noticed it was exactly the same shirt as the yellow one Shanice was wearing. Yellow used to be *their* color, Mira and Shanice's.

"Thanks," Chloe said, and started talking about the day her mom had taken them shopping to buy them. That day had apparently involved hours of trying on clothes and giggling and nibbling on tiny sandwiches and frosted cupcakes with Chloe's and Shanice's names on them.

While Mira listened, she noticed that Chloe's yellow-and-gold hair barrettes matched the beads in Shanice's braids. Mira forced a smile. The morning was so perfect, she couldn't bear for it to be ruined by being jealous of Chloe. She managed to keep a smile on during the entire bus ride.

Once they arrived at school, the sight of the familiar buildings was so comforting that Mira floated into the office to get her class assignments, catching herself every so often walking on tip-toe in a happy daze. She wasn't in homeroom with Shanice, but that was okay; she had World History first period with her, and Shanice saved her a seat. Mira had to have a locker by herself, as everyone else already had locker partners, but that was okay too. Mira went gliding through the first few classes, saying hello to this person or that.

By third period, though, she began to notice how many conversations were about events she hadn't been present for: a strawberry-picking field trip, the school dance with the high school band, the time Gerald Todd brought his dad's clippers to school and buzzed the hair off all his friends' heads and got in-school suspension. She had missed so much of the school year! People talked and Mira listened. But she was on the outside of all the activity; there was an *in* place she couldn't reach. And Shanice's and Chloe's names were mentioned together so often, the names seemed to have merged: *Shanice'n'Chloe*. Mira kept that smile on her face, nodding, nodding.

At lunch, she learned the sixth graders here were required to sit by homeroom and already had permanent seats. Mira took the empty place next to Anthony Brent, who spent the entire period turned away from her, talking to his friends. In afternoon elective, Mira didn't get Advanced Dance Team with Shanice and Chloe. She hadn't been there for auditions and would have been far too behind, according to the counselor. Mira was assigned to regular PE, where the kids ran the track and she tripped on the laces of her glittery silver sneakers.

By the time Mira boarded the bus to go home, her elation had worn off. She was happy to be there, she was, only . . . going back to Western Prince didn't feel like the homecoming she'd expected.

She slid into her seat, holding on to the comforting warmth of her pendant, and looked out at the afternoon. A blue sky with not a cloud in sight. But the day didn't feel sunny. The seat next to her was empty. Shanice and Chloe had ridden the activities bus to the gymnastics center. Ridden off without her. Mira had watched the bus leave.

Maybe a gymnastics scholarship should be Mira's last wish. That way, her life would be the same as before. All her activities restored. Of course, she hadn't practiced all year and had missed so many competitions. She was out of shape and behind.

And . . . wasn't that a silly use for a magic wish, really? After-school activities?

It would be much more sensible to wish for a big box of gold. That would pay for gymnastics and a heap of other stuff. She'd simply specify that the box not fall from the sky onto her head, or otherwise injure her. That's all.

It still didn't feel like the right wish, though.

The bus was passing the Marathon gas station. In the parking lot, a woman in a pink top hat with exceptionally long hair—the ends of it brushed her ankles—was working a string puppet for a very attentive poodle.

She come up out of the pond, Mrs. Sutter's voice said in Mira's mind.

Mira shivered. It was funny, she thought, how quickly she'd gotten used to the astonishing fact that Lyndame had a real live wand that could grant real live wishes. Mira hadn't thought about it all day. But if the wand had real magic, what did that mean for Mrs. Sutter's theories about Glass Pond?

Mrs. Sutter had always claimed the people coming up out of the pond were magical, though she'd not provided evidence of that.

Behind the gas station was the tall privacy fence surrounding the pond. Mira had never seen the pond. Papa had said it was a regular old pond. Gammy said the pond was deep and had slippery edges and that Mira wasn't allowed anywhere near it. But what *did* Glass Pond look like?

After Mrs. Jackson dropped her off at the house, Mira went inside for an apple, then came out to sit on the front stoop to eat it and think.

The turtle that lived on the corner ambled across the yard in front of her, taking his sweet time traveling to the house on other side. He was headed to dine on the mushrooms under the dogwood tree, she knew. A long, lonely journey. He was always by himself, that turtle. She wondered if he was happy like that. A good while later, the turtle was munching away.

Mrs. Sutter would soon be ambling over to the house. Knowing Mrs. Sutter was coming was kind of like anticipating a shot at the doctor's office or realizing you'd accidentally touched poison ivy and would soon break out in spots. An unavoidable, unpleasant truth.

Mira had finished the apple when the elementary school bus creaked and groaned around the corner, stopping a few houses down. Kids streamed out. Mira caught a glimpse of Sara's blond hair.

"BYE, Y'ALL!" Sara screamed to a group of girls who were headed in the opposite direction.

One of the girls waved half-heartedly, and none of them turned around. Sara seemed to slump.

Partway down the driveway, Sara noticed Mira sitting there. "I'm really popular at this school," she said, and plastered on a smile.

Mira nodded. Sara had cut her own hair again, she noticed, the bangs much too short and uneven. Even with Sara's delicate features, they did not look good. "You know, those bangs . . ."

And Mira was about to say *need some work*. And she was going to offer to help, comb them to the side or put gel on them, and was going to give some advice about how sometimes you should just try to fit in. But at Mira's first few words, Sara's big smile slipped and Mira caught a glimpse of what was underneath: a *real* Sara who was not happy in the least, who might actually be deeply unhappy.

". . . are really awesome," Mira finished. "They're so trendy. Who's that celebrity with bangs like that? I can't remember her name."

Sara got a hopeful gleam in her eye. "Zeebee!" And she

launched into a description of someone who might have been an actual person or might have been a character from one of Sara's graphic novels. The younger girl sat so close next to Mira that their legs touched. Mira felt crowded but resisted the urge to scoot away.

She just let Sara talk. It felt right to do that.

Chapter Eleven

I got me some interesting news today," Mrs. Sutter said the moment she walked into Mira's house. The woman didn't even start on her normal arrival activities: straightening the kitchen (poking her nose into the refrigerator) or freshening up in the bathroom (rifling through the medicine cabinet). She just stood in the family room, staring at Mira like she'd never seen her before.

Mira had already armed herself with her book. She scrunched down into Papa's chair.

"She come up out of Glass Pond!" Mrs. Sutter said it like it was a major announcement, clicking her dentures excitedly.

Mira was curious in spite of herself. "Who? The woman with the puppet?"

"Not her. My cousin's friend Ezekiel's son told it. He used to work for Mrs. Martha. Enlisted, though, and just came back from his third tour and he told his mother, Judy."

Mira was having trouble following. "Ezekiel's son came from Glass Pond?"

Mrs. Sutter's head went back and forth, like she was watching a tennis match. "Not him. He's the one that saw it. Mrs. Martha aids them that come up out of Glass Pond, he says. Gets them a bite to eat, some donated clothes. Don't none of them people belong here. Some mean to come. Some don't. And today I heard about one that come out, oh, twelve or thirteen years back."

"Okay," Mira said. Her head spun a little.

"You ready for this?" Mrs. Sutter paused dramatically.

"I guess . . ." Mira said.

"It was *your momma*! Your momma come up out of Glass Pond." She accompanied the proclamation with a shaking finger pointed at Mira.

Mira put down her book. The woman had gone too far. Mira glared. "My mother was a home inspector, and Papa's job was treating houses for termites. She ended up recommending him for all her houses, even those that hadn't seen a lick of termites. Because she liked him." Mira remembered Papa telling her that, the corners of his eyes crinkling at the memory, his crooked smile.

Mrs. Sutter's eyes lit up behind her glasses. "She just worked for them home inspector people, sounds like. They hired her after she come up. She needed a job, she did."

"I don't believe you," Mira said. Papa would have told her something like that.

"Your momma come up, but she didn't go back like the rest of them do. When they're ready, they just give a jump and go on back in. Water sorta reaches out to get them. A sight to see, Judy said, gave her son the shivers. She says it's the reason he enlisted."

Mira imagined water reaching out to get someone. She got the shivers too.

"Don't suppose you want me to tell her," Mrs. Sutter said, shifting her hips.

"Tell who what?" Mira said.

"Tell Val where your mother was *really* from. She'll probably decide to ship you off at that. Danger to those other kids, I bet."

Mira's heart dropped to her toes. She didn't want to ask, but she had to know, and when her voice came out, it was small. "Ship me off to where?"

"The system. You know, foster care, a group home, a facility, what have you. You never heard of such, girl?"

Mira had. She just never thought they applied to her. She had a house, didn't she? She stood abruptly. Her book fell to the floor.

As if Mrs. Sutter knew what Mira was thinking, the woman said slyly, "Too bad it all goes to the wife when the husband dies. The house, all the money. Surprised you, have I?"

The faintest rustling from the hall. Sara was spying on them, Mira realized. She'd thought Sara was playing outside.

"No, you haven't," Mira said through gritted teeth. She marched to the front door.

"Aw, don't be like that, girl," Mrs. Sutter said. "I'm just trying to help you out. Gotta face facts, don't you?"

Mira wasn't sure those *were* the facts. Her mother appearing out of a pond was outrageous, far-fetched, utterly ridiculous. And gossipy old women weren't the most reliable source of information, Mira knew. She walked out the door without any plan for where she was going, ignoring Mrs. Sutter's calls to return. Blinded by the afternoon sun, Mira stumbled a little on the front steps and made her way with difficulty up the sidewalk. She just wanted to put some space between her and Mrs. Sutter, and quickly. She was barefoot and the pavement was hot; she trekked through the grass to cool her feet whenever she could. At the end of the street, she marched onto Nunnelly Farm Road and soon was on New Hope Church Road.

The postwoman tooted her truck's horn as she passed by and Mira waved. *Don't mind me*, she thought. *Just out for a stroll.*

Caw! Bandit was flying tree to tree as Mira walked, following her, likely curious about where she was going.

Mira hadn't known where she was going until she reached the intersection with I-78 and stood at the crosswalk, waiting for the light to change, a stiff wind blowing sideways, whipping her cheeks with her hair. She wasn't supposed to cross the highway by herself. It gave her a thrill of fear.

In the Marathon gas station parking lot, a man in colorful striped socks hunched between the dumpster and the clothes donation bin for the Children's Hospital. He wore a cardboard box on his head and appeared to be sleeping. Mira didn't want to disturb him. She picked her way across the hot parking lot to the Between Grocery. *We appreciate your business!* the sign said. The chime sounded and the door didn't quite close behind her, letting in a breeze that ruffled the curly hair of the teenager behind the counter.

"Is Mrs. Martha here?" Mira said.

"Nah, she's gone home," the boy said. His gaze went to her feet. "You know you got no shoes on?"

"I know," Mira said. "When will Mrs. Martha be back?"

"Tomorrow. She comes in real early."

"Does she help people that come up out of Glass Pond?"

The boy did a double take. His expression turned suspicious. "You don't look wet to me. And I seen you here before with your pa. What're you trying to pull?"

He thought she was trying to claim that *she'd* come up out of Glass Pond, Mira realized. Did that mean people came into the grocery dripping wet on regular occasion? "Are you saying people *do* come out of the pond from somewhere else? They really do?"

His face closed off. He made a show of reorganizing a display of deodorizers. "Look here, 'less you got money, you plan on buying something, you need to move on. Mrs. Martha says no lingerers."

Mira's eye was a caught by a small movement in the produce-and-snack aisle. "You mean to tell me that lady is buying something?"

An ancient woman in a gauzy turquoise dress sat on an upturned peach crate, reading a small leather book. She gave Mira a little wave.

The boy leaned forward. "Smart girl, are you? For all your smarts, you seem to be forgetting"—he pointed at her feet—"no shoes, no service. Now, you get on out of here."

Mira had somehow made a bad impression on this boy. "Um,

I'll come back tomorrow."

"You do that. I'll tell Mrs. Martha you were asking after her."
It sounded vaguely like a threat.

Mira walked outside and paused in the parking lot. If she
was coming from the pond, which way would she have come?
Mira went around to the back of the store. Yes, there was a well-
worn path toward the fenced pond. A path that wound between
evergreen bushes and trees. She followed it, gingerly avoiding
prickly sweetgum balls and red ant nests. The path dead-ended
at the fence, at a gate with no handle, only an old iron plate like
someone had removed the latch, or maybe the latch was on the
other side. She put her eye to a crack between the slats. Weeds
and more weeds. She turned around in frustration.

The ancient woman in turquoise was standing there, smiling; although she didn't have many teeth to smile with. She was
very short—the top of her head was level with Mira's chin—and
now that she was closer, Mira could see the gauzy dress looked
to be made of hundreds of fluttery *leaves*. That, combined with
the woman's incredibly wrinkled skin and short cap of hair, both
the color of bark, made it seem like she'd just stepped out of an
oak tree.

Mira moved back a pace. "You scared me."

The woman extended a bony finger to Mira's pendant.

Mira covered her pendant with her hand. "Why are you
pointing at my necklace?"

The woman spoke a few words. It was a language Mira didn't
understand. The woman seemed to be asking a question.

"I'm sorry, I don't know what you're saying," Mira said, edging around her.

The woman continued to talk, raising her voice as Mira hurried away. When she reached the building, Mira peered back down the path, but the woman hadn't followed her.

Where had the woman come from? Could she have come from the pond? Why did she point at Mira's necklace?

There were those to whom Mira could have posed her questions. Those whose answers she would have trusted.

But of course, those people were no longer here.

Chapter Twelve

Just north of the Marathon gas station, beside New Hope Church and across the road from the Meeting Hall, was a graveyard. No fence separated it from the road, only a few feet of scrubby grass and a sign: *Families are responsible for upkeep and cleaning their respective gravesites.*

Mira walked in the soft grass beside the asphalt path. It took her a few minutes to find the markers—it had been over a year since she was in the spot.

Three stones, all in a row: Mira's mother, Gammy, and Papa. Someone had weeded. Papa's grave had a cactus plant on it.

Mira had been much too young to remember her mother's graveside service (Had her infant self even been invited? She didn't know), but she remembered Gammy's and Papa's all too well.

And those were memories Mira wished she didn't have. People standing around stiffly. The smell of that freshly turned dirt. The wind blowing grit into Mira's face—she didn't remember which service that had been, maybe both. The sickly sweet smell of the roses the funeral man gave her to throw in. After Gammy.

After Papa. Mira hated roses now. The funeral man tossed dirt over the polished caskets. It didn't seem possible that anyone could be in those fancy boxes. Much less the people Mira loved most of all.

Mira hadn't cried at Papa's service. Maybe because it'd been a short ten months since Gammy's, and Mira had cried out all her tears then. At Papa's service, Mira had been dry as a bone, dry as a desert floor—there didn't seem to be a single tear or even a drop of water inside her body. People tried to hug her, she didn't remember who, but she was like a mummy of herself, too stiff and dried up and her dress was too tight and she was unable to lift her arms or react to the hugs in any way.

Val had been the exact opposite. Val acted like all the sadness in the world was hers the day Papa was buried. She cried and cried, hanging on to her friend Abbie, squeezing Sara and Beans, who also cried buckets, their faces pink and puffy. They hadn't known him long enough to cry like that, Mira thought. How long had Val and Papa dated before they got married? Six months. Six months was nothing.

Mira stared at the markers now. Life was so fragile, wasn't it? The smallest thing could ruin it: the bacteria that invaded a cut on her mother's hand and traveled to her heart. The tiny blood clot that made a stroke in Gammy's brain. The trucker who made a slight miscalculation at the wheel that caused Papa to swerve and hit the tree.

It made no sense to love people, Mira thought, no sense at all, because it was too easy for them to be gone.

Papa had not been a formal person. Most people had called him Charlie. But his stone made him sound formal:

CHARLES MORRIS BLAISE

OCTOBER 25, 1981–APRIL 8, 2017

The one-year anniversary of Papa's accident had been last month. Mira had sleepwalked through the day.

A passing truck driver honked his horn and Mira jumped.

This wasn't a very restful resting place.

"I hope you can sleep here. I hope you don't worry about us," Mira said. "I love you, Papa."

On the next marker was Mira's own name—the name she and Gammy had shared:

MINA MIRABELLA BLAISE

JANUARY 12, 1950–MAY 30, 2016

"I hope you don't worry either, Gammy. I miss you so much." Mira kissed the top of her fingers, then blew the kiss to Gammy. It was the way they'd always done it. Mira would run out to the bus stop and look back to see Gammy blowing kisses from the doorway, and Mira would blow kisses back.

And then there was her mother:

AISLING BLAISE

RETURNED TO OUR FATHER

MARCH 17, 2007

Mira put a hand to her pendant. "Thank you for leaving me this. And thank you for having me as your daughter. I wish you could've stayed, though."

She studied the stone. There was no birth date, Mira noticed.

Not like Gammy's and Papa's, which included *both* birth and death dates. No middle name either.

Mira wondered if Papa hadn't known either of those things. He hadn't seemed to know very much about her. Mira had liked asking about her mother because the old answers were comforting: *She loved being in the garden. I'd see her out there, smiling to herself* and *You should have seen how many flowers she planted. So many colors!* and *She loved to watch you sleep. She could watch you for hours.* But now those statements didn't seem very satisfying. Why had Papa not known more?

The longer Mira considered it, the more her mother *did* seem like a woman of mystery. A woman who could have come from anywhere. A woman who could have come up out of Glass Pond.

Don't suppose you want me to tell her.

That statement made it sound like Mrs. Sutter was going to do exactly that. And would that be the last straw for Val? Val was protective of her daughters. Even if Val couldn't be sure what Mrs. Sutter said was true, would she ship Mira off to protect Sara and Beans? Mira wondered what it would be like to be shipped off. She pictured herself on the stern of a ship looking back, getting smaller and smaller as the ship sailed away, until there was only a tiny blip of Mira left, and then the ship would sail over the horizon and there'd be nothing left of Mira at all.

"Is there something I should know? Did you keep a secret from me?" she asked Papa, Gammy, her mother.

The wind blew through the stones. Mira listened hard, and then . . .

Caw!

She flinched. Bandit was perched on a gravestone nearby.

It was all the answer Mira was going to get from here.

"That was obnoxious!" Mira said to Bandit, louder than necessary. "I ought to give your peanuts to the squirrels!"

Bandit squawked and flew indignantly into the trees. Mira marched to the street, though her footsteps slowed the closer she got to home.

At the house, Val's blue Kia was parked at the curb.

Sara waited on the front stoop. She came to greet Mira at the street. "Mrs. Sutter is a hiney-hole," she said.

"You're not supposed to call people that," Mira said.

"Mrs. Sutter might be a villain in disguise. You need to be careful."

"She's not very well disguised."

"Hey, if your mom was magic, does that mean *you're* magic? Magic people *definitely* get attacked by villains, usually supervillains," Sara said.

Yes, it was clear Sara had been spying, listening in on Mrs. Sutter's claims about Mira's mother. And it wouldn't matter if Mrs. Sutter told Val or not, Mira realized. Sara could not keep a secret. Mira sighed and walked past Sara toward the door. "You've been reading too many graphic novels. Leave me alone."

Sara frowned. "Maybe you haven't been reading *enough* graphic novels." She tore into the house ahead of Mira and slammed the front door.

Entering behind her, Mira found a furious Val, hands on

her hips. "Where on earth have you been? Mrs. Sutter says you walked out the door without a word to anyone. What were you thinking, doing something so unsafe? That is not like you! You're usually so levelheaded. I don't know what to do with you anymore. I don't know how to handle this."

Beans also scolded Mira. "You didn't say any words!"

"Hush, Beans, go get some crackers and watch television," Val said.

"Did she tell you about my mother?" Mira said to Val, glancing at Sara, who sat in a chair grumpily, arms crossed.

"Don't try to change the subject," Val said. "And let's not forget about this morning. We still have those clothes to talk about."

Mira glanced down at the miniskirt and polka-dot shirt she'd gotten from Lyndame. Mira had meant to change her clothes earlier in hopes that Val would forget. At least Mira had left the glittery sneakers upstairs, hopefully safe from being confiscated by Val. "No, I don't want to," Mira said. There was really nothing she *could* say.

"You've left me no choice, then. You are grounded, young lady."

Well, at least that meant she wasn't going to be shipped off directly. And really, how was being grounded going to make today different from any other day? Mira laughed ruefully.

"And now you're laughing at me? I cannot believe this behavior!" Val said.

Beans wasn't joining in on the scolding anymore. She hadn't

gone to watch television as instructed; she looked up at her mother fearfully. Probably she'd never seen Val's face so red before.

"No . . ." Mira said. She definitely hadn't been laughing at Val, but the fact remained that Mira *had* laughed.

"Go upstairs, this instant. Don't come down again until you're called. I am so mad with you right now I could spit."

Mira wasn't sure what Val could spit at her, but at that moment, it felt like it might sting.

She went upstairs as fast as she could.

Chapter Thirteen

Mira lay in her bed, quilt pulled up to her chin.

She was going to be sent away, she knew it. All the making herself useful hadn't been enough. Deep down, she'd known it wouldn't be enough. Even last year, she had known.

The cashier at Quality Foods had made sure of it.

Mira, Val, Sara, and Beans were shopping. Mira was unloading items from the cart onto the checkout counter. Beans was sitting in the cart, and Sara was pushing it. The cashier looked at the girls, at Val dashing up with the paper towels she'd gone back to get, and then at Mira. "That your family?" His tone was skeptical; he'd clearly noticed they looked nothing alike. Val was close enough to have heard that question, as well as Mira's automatic response, "No, I just live with them." And Val didn't argue, didn't correct Mira, didn't say: *Of course she's part of our family!* or *She might as well be my own daughter!* Val simply looked annoyed and said, "That is an inappropriate question," and muttered about people minding their own business. So, it turned out to be another test for Val, though Mira didn't plan it. Whether Mira meant to or not, she had spoken the truth: she just lived with them.

Sara was making shuffling noises at the top of the stair, not saying anything.

"I hear you over there," Mira said. "You might as well come in."

Sara slid onto the landing on her knees, hugging the newel-post. She was already wearing the fuzzy pajama pants and the tank top she liked to sleep in. It must've been pretty late. And her eyes were red, like she'd been crying.

"What's wrong with you?" Mira said.

"It's Beans," Sara said.

"What about her?"

"She says people fight too much here. That we're all mean. She wants to go live with the pixies."

Mira's head fell back onto the pillow. "There's no such thing as pixies."

"We don't know that for sure." Sara scooched closer, as if she was cleaning the floorboards with those fuzzy pajama pants. "I heard her, in Fairy Village earlier. She was talking to someone."

"She does that all the time," Mira said. "She's got those Sparkle Girlz out there. She keeps them in the ballroom."

"But I heard someone *talking back*," Sara said. "And it had this laugh. *Heh heh heh.*"

The hair on the back of Mira's neck prickled. "Don't do that." Sara couldn't have heard a laugh like that. "She was probably pretending that Fairy Village is a real village and made that voice herself."

"The pixies don't live in our village, Beans says. They just visit her there. They say if she comes with them for real and for always that she will dance in the center of their circle. That she will be queen of their barrow."

That *did* sound creepy. And faintly familiar. Like Mira had heard it somewhere before. "Beans must've seen that on television."

"I don't want her to go away forever," Sara said, sniffling. "She won't listen to me. Can you talk to her?"

"Me? She doesn't listen to me."

"Yes, she does," Sara said. "She always listens to you."

If that was so, it was because Mira was an outsider, she reminded herself. Like when she was little and thought that everything her babysitter Taddy Dee said was amazing and exactly right. "Talk to your mom. She can tell her not to go."

"Mom isn't going to believe me. Please, will you talk to her?"

"Yes, I'll talk to her," Mira said. "As soon as I'm allowed out of my room." And she did intend to do that. She simply didn't think it was all that urgent.

"Okay," Sara said, and crept back down the stairs.

Mira was very tired. She tried to bring back her anger at Val, at the unforgivable thing Val had done, but it was hard, for some reason, to feel much more than a creeping numbness.

She closed her eyes, and the image of the three graves slid across her vision. She wished she could forget it, make the image disappear. Really, she wanted to make a world where no one ever had to die, ever had to leave. Like pressing reset, she thought. Like with the streaming television when it loaded too slowly, seemed to get jammed up and stuck. Her life was jammed up, messed up. Wouldn't it be great if she could press reset on her whole entire life?

∗ ∗ ∗

A noise in the corner of the room. Mira opened her eyes. She'd been sleeping. It was still night.

Gammy. In her favorite red beanie, doing a crossword puzzle while she rocked. She frequently did this while Mira was sleeping, watching over her (Was that rocking chair still in her bedroom? Mira had the vague impression that it wasn't).

The creak of the rocker on the floorboards must've woken her. "Gammy, is it you?" Mira said, sitting up in bed.

"Yes, my darlin'," Gammy said, still focused on the crossword. She'd forgotten her book light, Mira noticed. She was working the crossword by moonbeam.

Mira blinked. She felt like she had something important to ask but couldn't recall what it was, so she said, "Is that a hard one?"

"To be sure. It's from Sunday's paper. But problems are always hardest right before you figure them. Have you noticed?"

"Are you talking about the crossword?"

"Yes. And no."

Mira glanced around. There was the bookcase Papa had built, the stag Papa painted when she was into Bambi, the frog she created with tissue paper in Mr. Waller's preschool. But something was wrong. Somehow, she knew she couldn't be in her bedroom, although it looked like she was. She had moved to the attic, she knew that. Gammy's rocking chair was roughly in the place where the staircase should be. Mira must be dreaming. "You're not really here, are you, Gammy?"

A smile was in Gammy's voice as she studied her crossword. "No. And yes."

"You've left me. Everyone leaves." She sounded pathetic. But Gammy had always been one to comfort Mira; she didn't worry about sounding pathetic in front of Gammy.

Gammy looked at Mira then, and the moonbeam fell squarely on her face. That weathered face Mira had loved so well. "Are you sure, Mira? Are you sure everyone has left?"

Chapter Fourteen

Threads of dark clouds tainted the oranges and yellows of the dawn. Even though Mira still didn't know what her final wish would be, she put on her glittery sneakers along with a T-shirt and a well-worn pair of cutoffs and went out. The wind was cold and damp, the shadows dense, and the leaves rustled when she arrived at the ash tree.

Just inside the woods, Lyndame stood, legs squared, working the end of the plum braid. Edwin was perched high in a pine tree nearby, and he looked down his long bill at Mira.

"Did you come up out of Glass Pond?" Mira said.

Lyndame's brows went up. "And a good morning to you too."

"Did you?"

"What difference does it make where I come from, so long as I am granting you wishes of your choosing?"

Mira didn't know, exactly, what difference it did make, except . . . "I heard my mother came from there too. Did she?"

Lyndame didn't seem surprised by the question. "I would have thought your mother lived here. You have lived here always, have you not?"

She hadn't really answered the questions, Mira noted. "Wish grantors are usually tricksters trying to hurt you," she said.

"Is that so? How have you been hurt? I've faithfully granted what you wished for. I've even improved on your wishes. Come now, you must admit it."

It was true. So, why did Mira feel a churning in her stomach?

"It's not my fault you have not wished for, perhaps, that which is truly in your heart," Lyndame said.

Mira blinked. "I don't understand."

"You said, and I quote, 'I wish life was like before Papa died. I wish he were still here.'" Her voice was high and girlish.

Mira's cheeks grew hot. "That's not what I sound like."

"Yet that is what you said."

"But you told me I couldn't wish for Papa. You said it wasn't possible. That I needed to wish for an object."

"No, you cannot wish for him. But you need to think more creatively. Would a wish of your heart really be for frivolous things such as clothes or a particular school? Or would it be for a family?"

"A family," Mira repeated. "What do you mean?"

"What do you think I mean?"

"Somewhere I can belong," Mira said. "That's what family means." In spite of herself, she felt a tear come to her eye.

Lyndame smiled, showing those long canines. "Yes, that's it. Think about this: The wand could call to you a couple who desire children very much. A couple who would do whatever it takes to adopt a promising child such as yourself. The wand could locate them and create the proper paperwork to make them aware that you are here and . . . available. As you discovered with your last wish, words on paper can be a very powerful thing."

"Adopt me? I thought people only want to adopt infants. That's what the internet says."

"That's not always true."

"I thought you said we couldn't make anyone do anything. No compulsion, you said."

"There is no need for compulsion. There are couples who exist who desire a child exactly like you."

Mira's heart thumped. Here was a solution, presented in the nick of time. If Val was worried about where Mira's mother had come from, if Val found Mira too expensive, well, here was somewhere Mira could go, somewhere she could be happy. And hadn't Lyndame more than fulfilled the other wishes? She had done what she promised. There had been no tricks.

"A family to treasure you, to cherish you, to hold no one above you. Is that not your heart's desire?" Lyndame said.

It was hard for Mira to catch her breath. "But . . . I would have to leave here?" She scanned Fairy Village, the screened-in porch, even the shed that contained Papa's dried paints, gardening supplies, deflated baby pools; it all seemed precious to her. She'd never lived anywhere but here.

"Yes, no doubt," Lyndame said. "Yet your life would be complete."

Mira had thought she wanted her old life back. Her former school, friends, activities. But maybe those things, even this house, weren't what was important. Maybe what Mira wanted was simple: to be in the arms of a family that loved her.

Mira brought back an image of Papa's dear face and tried to replace it with someone else's. Someone new. It didn't really work. But to have a family of her own! Where she *fit*. Maybe that was why the other two wishes hadn't really worked, hadn't been satisfying, why wishing for gold hadn't seemed like the right wish either. She truly wanted nothing more than a family. "I guess so," Mira said. "But why are you helping me? Why are you here?"

"Why can your happiness not be my reward? And you will be happy, will you not? Those inside that house, those you live with, they have made it clear you don't belong here anymore. Isn't that so?" Lyndame held out an arm for Edwin and whistled.

They *had* made it clear, Mira thought with a pang in her chest. At least, Val had.

It was a Saturday last April. Mira was getting ready to compete in the invitational in Woodstock. The mats were down, the equipment readied. Mira stretched and bounced on her toes, smoothed her costume, then smoothed her hair. Even getting glitter on her palms from the glitter hairspray was a reassuring part of her warm-up routine. She wasn't particularly nervous. Her squad was starting with beam and she was strong on beam. She chalked her hands. It'd be soon. Two more girls and then her. Up on her toes again, stretching the bottoms of her feet.

She glanced at the bleachers. Mira had driven in early with Val and the girls. Papa was coming directly from work, but his spot was empty. That was odd. Papa was usually there by that point. He liked to watch warm-ups, Mira's squad marching in.

Mira wasn't too worried, though. Papa had never missed a weekend competition. Even the time lightning had struck a tree, minutes before they needed to leave for the Lakeside meet, and a limb landed on the porch roof. Papa simply put a tarp over it and loaded her into the car.

He was probably parking. He liked to park his car in a distant part of the lot, so no one would park next to him and ding his car's door. Even though he'd traded in his fancy Camaro for what he called "a more practical" Nissan, he was still particular.

Nie, Mira's squad-mate, completed her turn on the beam, her hop with a split (a bit wobbly). Her acrobatics were sound. Nice dismount. Mira clapped and then checked the bleachers again.

Still no Papa. And there was only one girl ahead of Mira: Shanice. Mira gave her a double thumbs-up. She knew Shanice would be expecting her to watch and so she did, although she continued to sneak looks at the bleachers.

Perfect cartwheel. Shanice must be pleased. Then the turn. She was always so graceful. Mira felt the smallest twinge of envy.

Up in the stands, Val was talking on her cell phone. That was also odd. Val usually insisted it was rude to talk on the phone in the middle of a meet.

Mira was up now, chalking her feet. She was sweating, a lot. Maybe she *was* nervous.

What was this? Val and the girls were climbing *down* the bleachers. They didn't look her way. Val was still on the phone, nudging Sara and Beans along. They weren't trying to get a closer look at Mira's performance. They were leaving!

Mira's name had to be called by the announcer twice.

She tried to shut everything out and focus on the beam, but . . . she did not do well. The coach patted Mira's shoulder afterward, but he was disappointed, she could tell.

It wasn't many minutes later that Mira knew what had happened. That was because Shanice's mom and dad were hurrying her out of there, to the hospital, even though Mira and Shanice would be defaulting the floor exercises. Shanice's mom sped so fast, Mira's stomach hurt worse than ever, but by the time they reached the hospital and the hospital bed, Val was holding Papa's lifeless hand, tears streaming down her face, shaking her head, again and again.

Val had made it there to say goodbye. *She had made it.* Papa was still alive when she arrived at the hospital. Sara and Beans, too, had been able to say goodbye. Val told Mira through her tears that Papa's last words had been, *It gets bigger.* Which made no sense. Had he been talking about heaven? Val probably hadn't heard the words right. But Mira wouldn't know. Because *Mira wasn't there.*

All Val had to do was give some signal. Mira would have left the beam at once. The beam was not important compared to Papa. Nothing was important compared to Papa.

Val made excuses later: she'd been rattled, she hadn't

understood the gravity of the situation, she hadn't wanted to disrupt the meet, she hadn't *realized*. But those excuses didn't feel like truth to Mira. Even when Val said she was so, so sorry, Mira hadn't believed it. Because when it came right down to it, down to when Val acted on instinct, down to the most important moment of all, down to *real* life and death, Mira was not included—she didn't matter.

* * *

"Have you decided? Do you want the wand to find you a family?" Lyndame said.

"Yes, I do," Mira said.

"You are sure?" Lyndame said. "That is your final wish?"

Again, she seemed too eager, but Mira didn't understand why that eagerness bothered her. She reminded herself that Val hadn't wanted her, had kept Papa's last moments to herself, had just been stuck with Mira. Mira wasn't a part of their family. Not really. She could never be. She could not forget.

At that moment, a ray of sunlight made its way through the trees to touch its warmth to her cheeks. Mira took it as a sign. "Yes, that's my final wish," she said. "I want the wand to find me a family."

Chapter Fifteen

New Mom and New Dad were standing side by side when Mira opened the front door in response to the bell.

New Mom wore her long, brown hair in a casually messy (but somehow perfect) updo, along with a bright smile. New Dad had a beard, neatly groomed, and a matching smile. They were the same height, tall, with freckles and olive-green eyes like Mira, dressed in navy suits and armed with manila folders. Not fifteen minutes had passed since Mira made her last wish.

"Hello," they said in unison. "You must be Mira."

Mira shook their hands. They had nice handshakes—firm and warm.

Mira, too, was dressed in navy. A short dress that looked perfect with her glittery silver sneakers. Her hair was curled and smelled of that pumpkin spice. Lyndame had probably planned on them taking a family portrait right away.

Mira led them inside.

Val walked into the family room, sporting flowered pajamas, a coffee cup, and an extreme case of bedhead. "What is this?

Who are you? Who are these people, Mira?"

"New parents that are perfect for me," Mira said. *Not like you*, she might have added, but that would have been mean. Plus, she didn't want to be rude in front of New Mom and New Dad.

"You have got to be kidding me," Val said. "These are strangers! People can't march in here and lay hands on other people. No one is leaving here. Absolutely not."

"We completely understand your concern," New Dad said. "There is no need to be alarmed."

"We are not strangers," New Mom said. "We have been briefed on Mira's background, *thoroughly*. We understand her to a tee. Everything is prepared for her."

"We have the paperwork here," New Dad said. "We have made all the arrangements."

"Perfectly legitimate," New Mom said. "You'll just need to sign."

"Who arranged for this? Social Services? Who called them? I'm not signing anything!" Val was saying. She'd splattered coffee on her pajamas.

Sara and Beans, likely attracted by Val's shouting, were peering in from the hall.

Mira hadn't expected anyone to be upset. She was shipping herself off before Val could do it. Saving everyone the trouble. But probably Val was pretending. Like the time Mira had ordered a triple-scoop cone at a fancy ice-cream parlor when Gammy said Mira could order whatever she wanted. Mira was full after one scoop but kept eating and making *yum* noises because the ice cream had been expensive and Gammy hadn't ordered any for herself. Mira had felt guilty.

"I want to go," Mira said. "Don't you see? I'm going where I can fit." She put on a big smile to match those of New Mom's and New Dad's. Mira's mother was from a magical place. New Mom and New Dad were found using magic. It really did make sense.

"No," Sara whispered from the doorway.

"Mira's spot-on correct," New Mom said. "She fits perfectly with us. See . . . We even look alike."

"That we do!" New Dad's smile was extra jolly.

They did look alike, very much so, even down to the freckles, which was odd, now that Mira thought about it. How had the wand found such a close match so quickly? The thought made her uncomfortable. *It's just that you're so happy*, Mira told herself. That was why her stomach was churning. It was completely reasonable for the wand to find perfect parents in such a short time. It was magic, after all.

Val's cheeks were rosy dots, and her blue eyes could have lasered though walls. "Exactly what is going on here? This can't be a legal process. Did these people give you the clothes, Mira? Remember what I told you girls about strange people offering gifts?"

New Mom and New Dad exchanged glances. "Who's that I hear at the door?" New Mom said.

"I don't hear anyone at the door," Val said.

The doorbell rang.

"I'll get it!" Mira said.

It was a plump woman with cropped auburn hair and a badge pinned to her mauve sweater set: *HI! I'M TERRY FROM CHILD AND FAMILY SERVICES.*

"Hi," the woman said to Mira. "I'm Terry from Child and Family Services. I have some paperwork here for your family." And upon noticing the others in the room: "Hi, everyone. I'm Terry."

"I'm calling the cops," Val said. She was pressing numbers into her phone and her hands shook.

"There is no need for concern. I'm Terry," Terry said.

"This can be a difficult transition," New Mom said.

"Why don't you have a seat," New Dad said.

"I'm not having a seat!" Val said. And into the phone: "Hello? Hello? Hello? Crap, I've dialed the wrong . . ."

New Mom touched Val's shoulder. "Ah, now. Let's be calm, don't you think? Won't that be better? We can discuss this like rational adults." For a moment, New Mom seemed to sparkle, to glow, but Mira must have imagined that.

The change in Val was instant. She stopped muttering, stopped trying to use her phone. She blinked at New Mom.

New Mom had such a soothing tone, Mira thought. She had such a gentle way with people. Even Mira felt calmer.

"It's all going to be fine," New Mom said to Val. "Mira will have a new life. A very happy life. You won't need to worry about her anymore."

"I won't need to worry," Val said.

"Let's sit," New Mom said.

"Okay," Val said. And she sat stiffly on a chair, hands on her knees. Her eyes moved slowly to Mira. She seemed to strain to speak. "But your house . . . your special things. It's taco night."

Well, it *was* taco night. They all looked forward to it. But maybe it was time to move on to new meals at new houses. Mira shrugged.

"Taco night!" New Mom said. "We love taco night, don't we, Doug?"

"Guacamole, sour cream, spicy sauce," New Dad said. "Yes, we can get it all."

They did *not* do sour cream on taco night, and the sauce needed to be *mild*, but Mira could fill them in on the menu later. They seemed agreeable to most anything.

"But, Mira . . . the teal pan," Val said.

Terry patted Val's back. "Yes, the teal pan," she agreed.

Gammy's enamel pan. Mira did use that pan for the taco sauce. Every week, she used that pan. She made a big deal of having it clean and ready. Why did she do that?

Val seemed to be talking to Terry. "It's comforting to Mira since her father passed. We've tried not to change too much. It's like these rituals. The same seven dinners each week, the same breakfasts. Dishes go in certain spots."

Mira felt her cheeks grow hot. Rituals! She was being *helpful* making dinner and Val knew it! She was saving face, is what Val was doing. She must be ashamed that she'd depended on Mira to do so much. Mira marched toward the door. "I'm ready to leave."

"No," Val whispered to herself. "This isn't right."

New Mom set a hand lightly on Val's shoulder. "Oh, my dear, it *is* right. This is the best arrangement for Mira and you know it."

Val's stare became vacant. She was tuning out, was truly going to let her go, Mira thought. She was probably ready to move on too.

"Mom, don't let her do it," Sara said. "They can't do this."

"Do what?" Beans said, tugging on Sara's pajamas.

"Mira is leaving," Sara said.

"Mira, no!" Beans said. *Miwa.*

"Mira, do you need help gathering your things?" New Mom said, eyeing the girls in the hallway.

Mira did have belongings upstairs: her quilt, her photographs, her books. But maybe it was time to move on from that stuff. It made her sad remembering her life before. And all the doing things as she'd always done them—what Val was calling *rituals*—it wasn't going to bring Papa and Gammy back. Mira knew that now. She touched the pendant at her throat. "No, I've got what I need."

"Perfect!" New Dad said. "We can always have her items shipped later. No worries there. Here's our card with our contact information." Val didn't reach for it. So he laid it on the coffee table.

"It's all going to be great," New Mom said. "We'll bring her to school today. Her dad and I."

"Yes, we will," New Dad said. "No worries, all 'round. Mira

won't have to ride the bus anymore. We'll enjoy driving her to school. In fact, we can drive her to Western Prince this very morning."

"After we show her the new house, don't forget," New Mom said. "It's a wonder."

"That it is," New Dad said.

"Social Services approved," Terry added with a wink.

Val didn't say anything, not even goodbye.

"Mom, why aren't you doing something?" Sara said. "Why are you just sitting there?"

Beans erupted into a wail.

"It's okay," Mira said to Beans and Sara. "This is good for me. Don't be—" *Sad*, she was going to say. She didn't get to finish because New Mom and New Dad rushed her out of the house, Terry shutting the door behind them.

Even through the door, Beans's cries followed Mira down the front walk. And even when Mira was tucked into the back seat of a brown station wagon, smelling of new leather, she could *still* hear the smaller girl's cries.

Behind the car, Terry was walking off briskly behind a tree and Sara was shouting, "You shouldn't do this, Mira Blaise! You love us, Mira Blaise!" And she ran down the sidewalk after them with a fist forward in what Mira knew was a Battlegirl flying pose, except the fictional Battlegirl from Sara's graphic novels could actually fly.

". . . and we were wondering if you wanted to start back with gymnastics right away," New Mom was saying. She was turned all the way around in the front seat, looking at Mira with a radiant smile. "Or did you need a little break?"

Mira blinked at her. "I can start now," she said. "I don't need a break."

"Wonderful," New Mom said. "And is that your pet? I didn't know you had a pet."

Bandit was flying behind the station wagon. He let out a great caw, then another.

"No, he's a wild bird," Mira said. "I do like animals, though. Wild ones."

"We sure knew *that*," New Dad interjected with a little grin. "Wait until you see."

New Mom smiled at him indulgently. "Oh yes, Mira, we've got a big backyard for you," she said. "Bird feeders. A deer salt. Bat houses. You can enjoy all the wildlife you like."

"We also put a gymnastics bar in the basement," New Dad said. "And another television."

"You've got twin beds in your bedroom. For sleepovers. And your own bathroom." New Mom was back to beaming at Mira. She reached out and took Mira's hand. Her hand felt so warm. Her olive-green eyes shone.

"You have a dimple in the same place as me," Mira said. Just to the right of her smile.

New Mom smiled bigger, deepening the dimple. "I do, don't I? Isn't that wonderful? I can't believe how perfect you are for us. I can't believe how lucky we were to find you. We'll be the perfect family." She squeezed Mira's hand.

"Yes, we will," New Dad said. "Picnics at Lake Lanier, vacations in Orlando, holidays with all the trimmings. We'll do it all, won't we? Just the three of us."

Mira felt like her heart might explode with joy, and although a little voice inside her head whispered things like *There's no such thing as perfect* and *This seems too good to be true* and *Val was acting weird, wasn't she?* it didn't matter because Mira wasn't listening to the voice at all.

Chapter Sixteen

The house of New Mom and New Dad wasn't very far away. And it *was* a wonder, exactly as they'd said. A Cape Cod–style cottage with a white picket fence, coral-pink azaleas blooming out front. The inside smelled brand-new and was perfectly neat. No unwashed dishes in the sink, no piles of dirty laundry, no stray book bags or stained coffee cups or untied shoes in the walkway for everyone to trip over. The sofas were white. The tables were marble. Everything shone like a beautiful metal.

Mira took a deep breath. It was unfamiliar and somewhat plain, sure, but she would get used to it. Who couldn't get used to this? "I can still go to my school today? Western Prince?" Mira wanted to hear their answers again.

"Of course," New Mom said.

"You bet," New Dad said. "Lookie here, check this out." He walked on his hands, and his car keys fell out of his pocket and smacked the hardwood floor.

New Mom laughed. "Maybe what Mira should check out is her *room*." She pointed. "Last door on the left."

Mira dashed down the hall. Her bedroom was wonderful:

twin beds with spotless white quilts, a television, an adjoining bath with gleaming fixtures. Best of all, a picture window framing a view of a lush backyard. Mira took an enraptured breath.

"Time for breakfast!" New Mom called.

Back in the kitchen, Mira found a dining nook, the table set with three places, each with foaming glasses of orange juice, shining silverware, and glossy white plates. The plates held scrambled eggs, bacon, and wheat toast with strawberry jam. New Mom and New Dad were already seated.

"When did you have time to make all this food?" Mira said. They'd only been in the house a few minutes. She blinked and for a second, she had the feeling this was all wrong, that the room was merely a set on a stage, that the parents looking at her so brightly were actors in a strange kind of play . . . but then she shook her head, determinedly shaking the feeling away. New Mom and New Dad had obviously made the breakfast earlier so that it would be there when they got back. Obviously! The houses weren't very far apart, after all. "I could have helped," she said. "I know how to cook."

"We wouldn't dream of you cooking," New Mom said. "With us, you'll get to be a child, as you are meant to be. Sit, darling."

Mira sat and proceeded to eat a hearty breakfast, exchanging happy glances with New Mom and New Dad and every so often waving to Bandit out the window. Bandit was making a meal of the vegetable garden, which only made New Mom and New Dad smile more. When Mira finished eating, she said, "I could make place cards for us. With our names on them. For the table setting, I mean." Like those she used to put on the table back at home: *Papa. Gammy. Mira.*

"What a fantastic notion," New Mom said.

"I can't wait to see them," New Dad said, and he was gathering the plates and putting them into the dishwasher. When Mira tried to assist, he bent into a modest bow and said, "Please, allow me."

"Let's work on your attire for school," New Mom said. "I've got so many ideas. It's your first day with us. I want it to be the most special day ever." And she took Mira by the hand, and they went back to Mira's room and opened a closet that was bigger than any closet Mira had ever seen except on television. The closet was filled with unusual and beautiful clothes, including an entire wall of gymnastic leotards (some spangled!) and hair bows in all colors of the rainbow.

New Mom went to a row of hanging jeans and selected a stonewashed pair for Mira. She laid the pair on an upholstered stool, then went around selecting other pieces while Mira toured the closet. It was like being at a store.

"What do you think of this?" New Mom said. She dropped a fuchsia beret on her head, sticking out her tongue and crossing her eyes. They both laughed. New Mom then pointed out that Mira was walking around on her toes. Mira explained that it was a habit left over from gymnastics. Then New Mom tried walking around on *her* toes but said it hurt and she couldn't imagine how Mira did that. They laughed about that too.

Mira was overwhelmed but happy. She obligingly dressed in

the clothes that New Mom selected: the jeans; a white tee with long sleeves, lace at the cuffs; and a cropped taupe vest. Though there were lots of shoes in the closet, she was loyal to her glittery silver sneakers; she was beginning to think of them as a good luck charm.

New Mom combed out Mira's hair and Mira closed her eyes, breathing in New Mom's floral perfume. "Should we curl it?" Mira said.

"I think not," New Mom said. "It's lovely as it is. Your crowning glory." She stroked Mira's hair.

Mira had never thought of her hair as a crowning glory before. It had always just been something to put into a bun or a ponytail holder.

New Mom added a headband of pink and gray to Mira's look. Then she said, "And let's not forget the finishing touch." She opened a cabinet.

Inside the cabinet were racks of earrings and necklaces, tiny little drawers. Along the back was a mirror lit up like a Hollywood studio.

New Mom opened a velvet-lined drawer and took out a silver link necklace with a pendant. The pendant was a small heart made up of glittering rubies inside a larger filigreed heart of silver. "My mother gave this to me," New Mom said. "She told me this was her heart keeping mine safe. And now, I give it to you. That's me, and you." She gently touched the small ruby heart in the center.

"Oh," Mira said. Her hand rose to her own pendant. She

102

hesitated because she didn't want to hurt New Mom's feelings. "But I already have a necklace. I don't know if I should . . ."

"I understand that one is very important to you. I would never try to replace it. But maybe you could wear my mother's necklace on special occasions? On days very important for our new family, like this one? You can keep your pendant safe here in your closet, in the meantime." And she nodded at a black velvet bust stand Mira hadn't noticed until then. It was bare.

Mira would have to do it, she felt. Changing out the necklace was symbolic, is what it was. It represented leaving her old life behind and embracing the new one. And it wasn't as if she was abandoning the pendant. She could still wear it most days.

She unlatched her necklace and carefully hung the gold chain on the black velvet bust. The emerald-green pendant shimmered at her.

New Mom slipped the silver necklace over Mira's head and stood back to admire it. "Look there, in your mirror. I love it."

The two of them were reflected in the mirror, vibrant in the lights. Mira in her new, fashionable clothes and New Mom in her smart navy suit; their hair exactly the same shade. They smiled at each other, showing their identical dimples. New Mom looked so much like Mira, in fact, it made Mira's heart ache.

"If you feel like it . . . if it feels good to you . . . if it feels right . . . you can call me *Mom*," New Mom said.

Mira had never used the word before, not to refer to her own mother, but she smiled and tried it out: "Mom." She liked the way it sounded. She glanced down at the new pendant she wore.

The shining rubies of the small heart were tucked so tenderly inside the larger heart.

When she looked up, New Mom was gone.

Standing in her spot was Lyndame.

Chapter Seventeen

Mira stepped back in shock from the mirror, from Lyndame. "What are you doing here? Where's Mom?"

Lyndame snickered. "*Mom.* Listen to you. What a fool you are."

"Mom!" Mira called. Her voice echoed in the empty closet; the clothes had disappeared. She ran into her bedroom, then the master bedroom. The house was exceptionally neat and clean and . . . she noticed now . . . generic. Bedspreads smooth, pillows fluffed just so, bureaus clear of picture frames or personal items. Down the hall and into the kitchen dining nook. The table held only a plastic flower arrangement. There was no trace of their breakfast. "Mom! Dad!" Mira shouted.

A shiny brochure was on the kitchen counter. On the front was a picture of the cottage, complete with the picket fence and coral-pink azaleas. *GORGEOUS FURNISHED THREE-BED-ROOM OFFERED AT $479,999.*

"No, no, no." Mira ran outside, leaving the front door wide open.

On the stoop was a life-size cardboard cutout of a dark-haired man wearing a big smile along with his navy suit. He carried a giant golden house key and a sign: *THIS COULD BE THE KEY TO YOUR FUTURE LIFE! BUY FROM DOUG!*

The cardboard cutout man looked a lot like New Dad. The man had the same jolly smile. "Dad?" Mira said. She backed away, nearly falling down the stairs of the stoop. And turning to the street, she found a large *FOR SALE* sign at the brick walk.

Lyndame stepped out the front door.

Mira stared at her. "They weren't real," she said. "You invented them." How was that even possible?

Edwin flew down to land on Lyndame's shoulder. "Just as you wished," Lyndame said.

"That is not what I wished for!" Mira said. "I wished for actual parents. Not for fake ones! Not for *you* being a fake parent. It was a trick. You tricked me."

Lyndame casually leaned against the doorframe. She petted Edwin with one hand and touched her throat with the other.

She wore Mira's pendant.

Mira gasped.

"Yes, I suppose I did trick you. Pretty creative of me, eh?" Lyndame said. "Took some doing to get the amulet off you, but I got it in the end. You had to be the one to remove it, you know. A powerful magic on that one."

Mira touched her neck. As expected, her pendant was gone. The silver necklace was still there, but it was a lie. She tore it off and threw it to the ground. "I had to—*why* would you do that? Why would you steal my necklace?"

"You should have just given it to me, like I asked. We're related, after all. You're my niece. Little bitty Mira. Course, no one knows your name."

Astonishment and a rush of unexpected joy. "I'm your . . . what? You're *related* to me?"

"Your mother was my sister. Not that I knew her, not really. She was a *much* older sister, to be sure. I came here looking for my sister, but I found you instead. Imagine that." Lyndame's lips twisted.

"But . . . you found your family. Isn't that good? Why don't you seem happy?"

"I'm very happy. It's very good. I'll be bringing you back to my mother exactly the way I always dreamed of bringing back my sister."

"But . . . why not just ask me? I would have gone with you if you'd asked. I would have definitely wanted to meet my . . . Are you saying I have grandparents?"

"A grandmother. Shame you'll never get to meet her, though. Now that you have no protection." And Lyndame smiled then, those canines flashing, and she took the wand from her sleeve, and the magic pulsed in the air, and the bird Edwin unfolded that violet crest and screamed.

"What are you doing?" Mira said.

"Doing away with *you*," Lyndame said. "Forever!"

Lyndame meant to *kill* her, Mira realized with sudden horror. "No! Help! Help me!" Without thinking, she charged at Lyndame. Mira aimed for her necklace, to take it back, or maybe the wand, to knock it from Lyndame's hands—Mira wasn't sure.

Events were confusing after that. Lyndame was waving the wand triumphantly, and sparks of light cut the air. Mira was crying out wordlessly, and there was a raucous cawing from Bandit and the rushing of wings and more screaming by Edwin. There were growls and grayish fur in the corner of Mira's vision, and Mira felt she nearly had her hands on her necklace, but Lyndame shoved her away and Mira tumbled backward, landing on her rear and hitting the back of her head on the bricks. *Whump!*

* * *

Mira was under her quilt, the mattress hard and uncomfortable. The floor went *creak creak*. Gammy was across the bedroom in her red beanie, rocking in the moonlight.

"Gammy?" Mira said, sitting up.

"Six letters across, *m* in the third spot . . ." Gammy murmured, intent on her crossword.

The mattress was *really* uncomfortable. But that made sense, Mira noted, because it wasn't actually a mattress. It was a flat white expanse dotted with familiar-looking plastic stars and an iridescent plastic moon, faintly glowing. And there was the lotus light fixture Papa had painted pink.

Mira looked up. Over her head was her bed, complete with her pillow. Also, her desk, her bureau, and her bookcase. It made her feel dizzy. She was on the ceiling. She and Gammy both. The bedroom was upside down. Or they were.

"Gammy, why are we up here?"

Gammy didn't glance up from her crossword. "Sometimes approaching a problem from a fresh angle is what you need to do. You might notice something you've not noticed before."

"Like how many dead moths are in this light fixture?" Mira said.

"Just so. Something that's been there for ages you've not paid attention to. It could be important."

"Dead moths are important?"

"Fresh angles are important. Looking at life from a different perspective. Maybe someone else's perspective. Don't forget, my sweet." And Gammy put aside the crossword with a small smile and rose from the rocker. A blanket slipped from her lap.

And then the room flipped over.

✳ ✳ ✳

Mira was falling, yelling. She jerked up to a sitting position. She was on the brick walk, in front of New Mom and New Dad's house, dizzy, the back of her head throbbing. She must've blacked out for a moment when she hit her head.

She blinked, trying to focus her vision. Lyndame was lying back against the stoop, as if she, too, had fallen, and the bird Edwin was standing on the ground hissing, head lowered and wings up.

Lyndame was staring in shock and dismay at a place over Mira's shoulder. Mira looked too.

Bandit was perched on the white picket fence. He held the wand in his bill, and his head turned this way and that, as if he admired the way the wand sparkled in the sunlight.

Well, Mira thought, that *is* the ultimate stick.

In front of the crow were gray foxes, an entire family of seven. Mira had never seen them all together or even out of the woods in the daylight. She recognized some of the smaller ones from last year's pups. Hackles raised, ears flattened, they growled at Lyndame. A small one yipped.

They were helping Mira. Why?

"This isn't over," Lyndame spat. And, scrambling to her feet, she ran off, pursued by a flapping Edwin and the larger of the foxes.

* * *

It took a few moments for Mira to collect herself. But she realized she needed to get the wand from Bandit, and quickly, before Lyndame returned. That wasn't going to be easy. Bandit wasn't the most gracious about sharing his spoils. He'd never returned any of her pencils, and she had no idea what he did with them.

The task was a distraction. A welcome one. Tears pricked Mira's eyes as she raced after Bandit. New Mom and New Dad had seemed so real to her. Or she had wanted so badly for them to be. Deep down, she'd suspected something wasn't right. But it felt impossible that they hadn't been alive, not ever. It seemed more like Lyndame had killed them, murdered them in cold blood, and Mira didn't actually know what it meant to have your blood be cold, but it sure did seem like Lyndame had blood like that.

Bandit's flying was erratic, big arcing swoops. He was weighted down by the wand. He landed on a branch of the fig tree at the corner.

"I need that!" Mira said to him. She didn't plan on using the wand. She didn't even know if she could. It would just be ever so much better if she had it instead of Lyndame. Lyndame had somehow used its magic to create walking, talking people. Clearly the wand could do much more than grant wishes of *medium size*. Mira felt so stupid for having believed that, for having believed in wishes to begin with. The wishes were an invention of Lyndame's, Mira suspected. A scam that Lyndame had created to get Mira's pendant. The wand was a powerful object, Mira believed now. It could probably do magic of all sorts.

And Lyndame had said Mira was her *niece*. She'd claimed they were family. She'd claimed Mira had a *grandmother*. Could it really be true?

The crow flickered the wand in the sunlight, like he was teasing her with it. Or could he be *aiming* at her? It wasn't all that funny, but Mira laughed out loud. She barely recognized the laughter; it sounded like a sob.

"Give it to me," Mira said. "Right now!"

But there, Bandit was flicking his head back and forth, and it seemed like he was simply enjoying playing with the wand, as if he wasn't so much teasing her as he was impressed by the shiny nature of his treasure. He spread his wings and resumed his flight.

A red-shingled house caught Mira's eye, and she realized she was on Belmont Drive, very close to her house.

Bandit landed on a roof across the street and then, after taunting her some more with the wand, he flew directly over the house and above the trees of the backyard.

Mira went headlong after him, plunging through someone's garden, accidentally stepping onto a patch of daylilies, and then dashing into a random backyard filled with plastic toys. But then there was a fence with a barking terrier inside, and she had to go around. Breathing hard, she emerged onto Lexington Drive.

"Where are you? Where, where?" Mira said.

She had lost sight of the crow *and* the wand.

Chapter Eighteen

Mira searched the skies for Bandit.

A flash of light in her side vision, in the upper branches of some pines. Had that been the daylight reflecting off the wand? The trees were right past her house.

When she dashed in that direction, she found Sara sitting on the front stoop.

"Oh, so now you decide to come back," Sara said.

Mira stopped to catch her breath, peering over Sara's head, up and over the house, squinting at the horizon, searching for the crow. "Well, it's just that Bandit . . . and what happened was . . ." How could she explain? New Mom and New Dad and the magic. Lyndame's treachery. The possibility that Mira had a living grandmother . . . It was all too impossible to believe. "Um, why aren't you at school?"

"Doesn't matter. You've done it now. It's a perfect disaster and it's all thanks to you," Sara said, standing.

"I did . . . what?" Mira said, focusing on her.

Sara was wearing the Zoo Atlanta T-shirt they'd bought on a trip with Papa; her favorite shirt—it was yellow and printed with the image of a tree frog. Her hands were fists. "Beans went to live with the pixies! You said you would talk to her, but instead you just left us here! And now Mrs. Sutter is *watching* us supposedly, but she's really watching *Judge Judy*, and Beans went out to Fairy Village and now she's gone!"

"Where's Val?" Mira said. Val had let them stay home from school? Val *never* did that.

"How should I know?" Sara said. "And what do you care? You with your fancy new clothes and fancy new life." She glared at Mira.

A few days ago, if Sara had insisted Beans ran off with the pixies, Mira would have assumed it wasn't true. But after all that had happened . . . "I believe you. Pixies are probably real. I've got to find a wand and then we can look for Beans."

Sara's mouth dropped open.

"Come on!" Mira said, and she was running again. Down the side of the house, past Fairy Village, and into the back. She felt sure Bandit would be somewhere in the woods.

"Wait!" Sara said from behind.

Where would Mira go if she was a crow?

She'd often seen Bandit harass the owl who roosted in the water oak, cawing at him and chasing him around. Yes, she'd try there. Mira hurriedly crunched through fallen leaves and pine needles while trying to keep an eye out for copperheads.

"What wand? Where are we going?" Sara called.

"I'm looking, give me a minute," Mira said, scanning the branches of the oak. Only a blue jay and an annoyed squirrel.

The owl must be off somewhere. And Bandit wasn't there.

"Tell me what we're looking for," Sara said.

"Just let me think," Mira said. Where else had she seen Bandit? On Nunnelly Farm Road, last week, picking at a dead possum. She hurried around scrubby bushes and vine-draped trees until at last she popped out on the other side of the woods at the spot where Bandit had been last week. But today there was no sign of the crow and no roadkill either.

Sara was breathing hard as she emerged from the woods. "What are we doing? *How* is this helping us find Beans?"

"Bandit has got the wand," Mira said, and panic invaded her chest. "I've got to get it back from him. I don't know what she'll do to me if she gets it first." She reached for the warmth of the pendant at her throat, for comfort, but of course it wasn't there.

"Who is *she*? Who are you worried about?"

"Let's just find the wand first and then I'll explain. It's urgent!" Mira said.

"Okay, okay. Well, I've seen where Bandit goes," Sara said.

Mira stared at her. "What do you mean?"

"Sometimes during the day, when I'm out here, I've seen a crow I'm pretty sure was Bandit. I'll show you."

Sara *was* always out in the woods, looking for frogs to put in jars. It might be true.

Back into the woods they went, Sara leading this time.

They hopped over a creek and hurried past the remains of someone's lean-to fort with a moldy flag, until at last they arrived at a stand of fallen trees.

"Around here somewhere," Sara said.

Mira stepped on an object before she saw it, half buried in the dirt: a yellow pencil, filthy and broken in two. "Hey, that's my pencil," Mira said, although she wasn't sure it was hers. It was just a standard number two pencil. But if it *was* one of her pencils, Bandit wasn't taking very good care of his stolen treasures.

"I hear something," Sara whispered.

Mira heard it too. A rustling, then a scratching.

On tiptoe, they followed the sounds.

Bandit was standing atop a rotten stump, prodding it with the wand. Scattered in the dirt: a second pencil, the flamingo swizzle stick Mira had seen him with, a lollipop stick (minus the candy), a ballpoint pen, a variety of straws, bent and twisted, and a toothbrush.

While Mira and Sara watched, Bandit fished out a fat grub—he'd speared it—and held the wand with his feet while he gobbled it down.

Mira could not believe it. The crow was using the wand as a *fork*.

"Argh!" she said, and lunged for the wand.

The crow squawked, startled.

When Mira seized the wand, when she finally had it in her hand, a clanging sound filled her ears. It was much louder than what she'd heard when Lyndame held it. This time it was not like a bell in the distance. It was more like a large dinner bell ringing right next to her, reverberating in her head. Nearby sounds were muffled: Bandit's caws of protest, Sara's exclamations, Mira's own gasp of surprise. And within the ringing sounds, there might have been something else, something like a promise . . .

Mira dropped the wand inside a fold of her shirt, and the sounds vanished. "Wow," she said.

"I heard it," Sara said, clearly impressed. "Where'd *that* come from?"

"I don't know. But there's this girl . . . a bad person . . . She was threatening me with this, so I know it's dangerous. I've got to hide it somewhere she won't find it." Without thinking, Mira tucked the wand inside her left sleeve. Actually, the wand seemed to tuck *itself* in there. Mira checked and yes, there it was, hanging out in her sleeve, fitting perfectly, attached like it was held by Velcro, like it was waiting for her to use it . . . not that she was going to try to use it, no matter how powerful the wand seemed. The thought of trying to use the wand, maybe in an attempt to recreate New Mom and New Dad, her perfect parents, her perfectly *fake* parents, nearly broke her heart in two.

"Roger that," Sara said. "You can fill me in later. Time to look for Beans. You promised."

Bandit was still on a branch above them, *caw-caw*ing and generally raising a ruckus.

After a moment's reflection, Mira removed her new pink-and-gray headband, tore the fabric, and extracted the stiff horseshoe-shaped piece of plastic inside. "What about this, Bandit? Maybe you could use this for digging?" She made a show of waving it around, then placing it on the stump.

Bandit gave it the once-over with a beady eye, then flew down to investigate.

"Okay, let's go," Mira said. "We'll look for clues."

"What are we looking for?" Sara said.

"Anything suspicious."

As they searched in the woods, Mira felt the weight of the wand in her sleeve. It was a powerful object, the wand—she felt sure of that now. There was much more it could do than grant a few simple wishes. And it might actually be possible for *her* to use that magic. That was the unspoken promise she'd received when she picked it up: the power of the wand was hers to command.

Not that she should use it. Of course she shouldn't. But now that she was thinking about it: *Why* did she feel, deep down in her bones, that she shouldn't? What would be so bad about using it?

Sara pounced on a small round object and held it up. "Look at this! This is suspicious, don't you think?"

"That's an old tennis ball missing the cover," Mira said. "Which probably rotted off."

"But *why* would someone be playing tennis in the woods?" Sara said. "Riddle me that, Batman."

"Throwing it for a dog?" Mira suggested.

"Yeah, I guess so." Sara tossed the remains of the ball over her shoulder. A moment later, she pointed out a cicada's exoskeleton on a tree. "Ah-ha! The insides must have been slurped out by ravenous pixies!"

"Cicadas molt and you know it."

"I know we've been *told* that, but what if it wasn't true and we were just told that to throw us off the scent?"

"Maybe. But it seemed like the zoo people knew what they were talking about. I doubt they're in league with the pixies."

Something caught Mira's eye and she bent to examine it: a Kelly green thread snared on a briar bush. "Is this the color of those socks Beans is always wearing?"

"Yes, it is! I'm sure because they used to be my soccer socks. Do you think Beans was passing by this way?" Sara said.

"Or maybe she's in there." Mira pointed at the large tangle of briars and weeds.

"Ah no. She couldn't have gone in there. She'd have gotten scratched to pieces. And it's full of snakes, I bet."

"I'm sure you're right," Mira said. She knelt and gingerly brushed away some dead leaves from the base of the plants. She didn't know what she was looking for.

"This is a waste of—what's that you've got there?" Sara said.

"Nothing. A rock." Mira had uncovered the base of a single square-cut piece of stone.

"Looks like a step."

"Could be more in there. It's hard to tell. We could come back with some gloves and clippers and dig it out. I guess." But why would Beans be inside a briar bush? They probably needed to go back to the house, to search around Fairy Village for clues.

"What about using the magic words?" Sara said.

119

"What magic words?"

"The ones Papa told us about the pixies. How'd they go again?"

Sara calling Mira's dad "Papa" had always grated on Mira's nerves. "Top of the morning to you," Mira said to the briars.

"No, not the greeting. The rhyme you say when you turn in a circle and all that."

Papa had demonstrated the rhyme and the method for calling the pixies to Mira when she was little. She hadn't known Papa shared it with Sara and Beans too. "That one is just a silly game for *little* kids," she said. "I played it with my *troll dolls*." Her tone was scathing; she couldn't seem to help it.

Sara was not put off. "Don't be mad. He only told us because we begged him for stories about Fairy Village. Please, please, please can we try it?"

"Why do you think it'd be helpful?"

"It calls the pixies, doesn't it? Don't we want the pixies to come? Maybe they'll bring Beans with them."

Mira breathed out noisily. "Fine!"

She stood and, feeling a little foolish, clapped and turned in a circle three times. And although she hadn't spoken them in years, she remembered the words of the rhyme easily. "Merry taker, mischief maker, thee of fae," she said. "Leave your barrow. Come out to play."

The two of them stared at the mound of briars.

Nothing happened. Bandit was making a racket in the distance, back to scraping away at the stump.

"See, I told you," Mira said. "It's just a silly—"

The faintest scuttling. And then a small voice: "Who is this who knows the rhyme? Who is this who carries the promise?"

A troll doll ducked out from under the briars in front of Mira and Sara.

Only it wasn't a troll. And it wasn't a doll.

It was a pixie.

Chapter Nineteen

The pixie was a slim, graceful figure no taller than a glass of water, wearing a velvet suit of moss green, a minuscule flower in the buttonhole. He had skin of the palest blue, slender pointed ears, and caramel hair that stood on end.

"Thee, I do not recognize," the pixie said, shiny black eyes taking in Mira. "Yet I made a promise to thee. I can feel it and am bound to it."

"I can't believe that really worked," Mira said.

"That never happened when *I* said the words," Sara said.

"Thee is much too large," the pixie said to Sara, sneering. "And I never made a promise to *thee*."

"I don't remember any promise," Mira said.

The pixie rolled his eyes then. He waved a tiny hand at her and chanted, "Memory bound by age and rhyme. Buried down inside thy mind. Childish memories soon to find. I command thee now, unbind!"

It was like a dam broke, like a fog cleared. The memories came flooding back so fast, Mira stumbled a little. And she knew something at once and with complete certainty:

She had never owned any troll dolls.

"I have restored thy memories," the pixie said impatiently. "Now thee must tell . . . how are thee in possession of a great magic carried in the sleeve? And why does thee search for fae?"

The pixie could sense she had the wand? Mira filed that knowledge away. "I'm Mira. Mirabella. You're Hipple . . . aren't you?"

"How does thee know my name? Thee does not look like anyone *I* know. When was this acquaintance made?"

"Don't you recognize me?"

"Not a whit. Not a smidgen. Not a speck. Thee is as strange as a vapor on a midsummer morn."

But Mira recognized him. And she remembered now. When Mira was very young, she had played with Hipple in Fairy Village, many afternoons in a row. The pixie promised to come when Mira called. If she clapped and turned in a circle three times when she called, he would come. She forgot it was real. For years, she had forgotten. Or maybe it was the spell, causing her to forget. But in any case, he'd kept his promise. "I've grown," Mira said. "I got bigger. It's still me. Remember Simon Says?"

Hipple gave her a long, skeptical look. "Thee *always* let me be Simon."

"No, I didn't," Mira said. "I never let you be Simon. I'm sorry about that, by the way. Remember the freeze dance, though? Knick knack, paddy whack, give the dog a bone . . ."

The change in the pixie's expression was dramatic. He barked a laugh and began an undignified jig, singing as he danced,

"This old man came rolling home. This old man, he played two, he played—"

"Freeze," Mira said, because she remembered Hipple was perfectly capable of going into double digits with that song and it was time to get back to their purpose.

"But that is not how the game is played," Hipple protested. "I was making the music. Only I may stop the music."

Mira exchanged glances with Sara. "We're looking for Beans."

Hipple's little face became cagey. "If thee wants beans, thee should look in a garden."

Sara sucked in a breath.

"Have you seen her?" Mira said. "Did she go with you?" Hipple had always wanted Mira to come back with him to the barrow, she recalled. But even as small as Mira was then, she knew better than to do that.

"To call for fae, thee must be pure of heart. Thee must have no ulterior motive," Hipple said, chin held high. He turned on his heel.

Mira dove and managed to grab hold of his jacket as she landed next to him. She was at an awkward angle and didn't have a good grip. He was going to wriggle out of his jacket, she could tell. And if he escaped, what would happen to Beans?

Sara was there. She took the pixie by the waist, holding him close to her nose. "Speak, villain! What have you done with Beans?"

Hipple stopped struggling. "No villain am I! The queen does what the queen wills."

Mira felt a stab of fear as she scrambled to her feet, brushing off her jeans. "Are you talking about Beans? Did you make her your queen?"

"There is nothing thee can say that will convince me to speak." Hipple made a deliberate zipping gesture across his lips. He then mimed locking his lips and throwing away the key.

"Hipple, we're friends, remember?" Mira said. "You can tell me."

The pixie moved his head slowly back and forth.

"Should I shake him?" Sara said. "Pull out his hair?"

Hipple glared at her.

"No, don't hurt him." Mira peered into the briar bush. "He came from inside those briars. We could get in there, if we bring back the clippers, but it'll take too long. It's practically lunchtime . . . ah, lunchtime, hmm." She focused on another memory that Hipple had freed with his spell, and turned to Sara. "Get that pouch he's got at his waist. Now."

A scuffle. Sara was grabbing for the pouch, and Hipple was wriggling free and dashing up her arm. He bounded down, shouting words in a pixie language that sounded like curses as he disappeared into the briar bush.

"Ow," Sara said, rubbing her nose. "He kicked me."

"Why'd you let him get away? We needed that pouch!"

Sara smiled and held out her palm. "This pouch, you mean?"

It was the tiniest of pouches, something that could have held a guitar pick, made out of poppy-colored leather and held together with a golden hook-and-eye closure. Mira squinted at it, gently fiddling with the closure. Inside was a teaspoon amount of what looked to be golden sand. "Stand back, okay? You don't want to get it on you. It's powerful stuff."

"What is it?" Sara said.

"Pixie dust," Mira said. She sprinkled a bit of the dust on the briars and recited: "Reveal to us that which is to other eyes concealed."

"Huh?" Sara said.

"I remember *so* much now. He used those words after he'd hidden his lunch from the squirrels. Just wait."

The briars glittered and twitched, shimmered and shifted, until they were no longer briars, but human-sized double doors set into the ground. Metal doors with peeling beige paint and rusted-out holes.

"Those don't look magical," Sara said. "They look like the doors to the nasty old root cellar our last landlord had."

"Help me with this," Mira said. And together they heaved open a door with a puff of dust and a squeal of rusty hinges. Beams of daylight fell onto stone steps leading down into a musty and damp dark space.

"It *is* a nasty old root cellar," Sara said. "Look, there's even some random mason jars someone left behind."

"Come on," Mira said.

They crept down the steps into the earth, blinking in the dim light, as broken glass crunched beneath their shoes. Stone walls, a dirt floor. A few of the mason jars were intact, but most were broken. Empty shelves gaped. A wooden chair was missing its seat.

"There's nothing here," Sara said. "Though it doesn't smell too bad, does it? It smells like . . ."

"Burnt sugar?" Mira said, and *that* memory was in her head too. "That's what they smell like."

"You mean they *are* here? Where are they?"

Mira shrugged and cleared dirt off a step. "Sit next to me." And then raising her voice, she announced: "We're not leaving here until you give her back. I know you can't get past us." At least, Mira didn't *think* the pixies could squeeze around the two of them with Beans in tow. Mira seemed to remember bumping into Hipple when she was small, once or twice, when they'd been playing tricks on Mrs. Sutter: hiding her newspaper and putting a plastic beetle in her mailbox and the like. Hipple had been covered in pixie dust and invisible, but he still had form and substance, she remembered, was still *there*.

No response but the chittering of a squirrel in the distance.

"We've got all day. All night even," Mira declared, poking at Sara when she made a sound of protest. "Yep. We can just sit here and wait. Oh, and recite nursery rhymes. We love those."

"We do?" Sara said.

They do, Mira mouthed. Because she had remembered that too.

"Jack Sprat could eat no fat," Mira recited. "His wife could eat no lean. And so, between them both, you see, they licked the platter clean." Mira thought she had done very well on that rhyme, her delivery nice and rhythmic, but the silence lengthened.

Sara mouthed *What?* meaning *What are you doing?* but Mira held up a finger to say *Wait* and started into "Ring Around the Rosie." She paused after "We all fall down."

The smallest sound could be heard from the shelves, like a dry leaf moved in a breeze.

"Can you sing something else?" Sara said. "That stuff is depressing. How about 'Battlegirl'?" The theme song, she meant.

Mira shook her head, then sang the lines of "Hey Diddle Diddle." When she finished, other tiny sounds had joined the first, and Sara had shut up, eyes fixed on the shelves. She had clued in to what Mira knew: the pixies found it hard to resist reacting to nursery rhymes.

Mira was full-on singing now, "All around the mulberry bush, the monkey chased the weasel. The monkey stopped to pull up his sock. *Pop!* goes the weasel." At the pop, she and Sara (following a half second behind) jumped up, hands raised.

A flickering at the shelves. A second stanza was beginning, the singing faint at first: "Half a pound of tuppenny rice, half a pound of treacle . . ." By the time the stanza was finished, a dozen small bodies danced and swung each other around and a dozen small voices were singing "Pop! goes the weasel" and starting over at the beginning of the rhyme. The gold and silver thread in the elaborate dresses and suits flashed in the spare light. The pixies, Mira remembered, were not only fond of dancing—they were very fond of their clothes.

While the pixies continued to sing and dance, Mira and Sara were feeling their way around the cellar.

"Here," Sara whispered urgently, seeming to pat the air in a corner.

Mira scattered the last of the pixie dust and quickly recited the words of the reveal charm.

Something shimmered into visibility. A mound of something the size of a bed pillow, curled up, sound asleep. As it fully appeared in all its pink-princess-dress-and-green-knee-socked glory, Sara cried, "Beans!"

Chapter Twenty

Beans rubbed the sleep from her eyes and got to her feet, adjusting a golden crown filigreed with flowers and dragonflies and studded with diamonds. She stood tall on the dirt floor of the root cellar, put her hands on her hips, and said, "I'm the biggest boss here, Mira and Sara. You have to do what I say. I'm the queen."

The way she said it made Mira feel sad, for some reason. Beans wore the golden crown the pixies must've created for her, sure she did, only her cheeks were smudged with dirt, the princess dress was torn, and her favorite green knee socks had more holes than ever. "Yes," Mira said. "You are large and in charge. A very important person, for sure."

Beans frowned, studying Mira's face, likely trying to figure out if she was being made fun of. But Mira had been sincere. The pixies had ceased their singing and were extending rapturous gazes in Beans's direction, nodding at Mira's declaration. It was clear the small girl *was* in charge here.

"You're queen of a root cellar?" Sara said.

"'Tis not *our* fault," Hipple said, sniffing. "Our barrow was demolished for a housing development."

"I'm queen of this place and all the places where the pixies are," Beans said.

"Long live the queen," the pixies said.

"May she ever grace our presence," the pixies said.

"Why did you come here?" Mira said to Beans.

Beans shrugged. "I ran away."

"Okay, but it's time to go home now," Mira said.

The pixies made sounds of protest, but they also watched for Beans's reaction.

With the toe of her shoe, Beans drew a circle in the dirt floor. And then another one. The pixies followed the movements closely. What had Beans done to make them love her so much? "I want avamacados on my taco," Beans said finally. Avocados, she meant. She had asked for those before, on taco night. But Papa hadn't liked avocados and Mira hadn't wanted to add them. Why would Beans think of that now? Mira studied her.

"You ran away because you want avocados?" Sara asked for them both.

The pixies were murmuring about these mysterious things called avamacados.

Mira was thinking: *I don't know if I'm having taco night with you anymore. I don't even know if I have a home with you anymore.* But she didn't want to say those things. She didn't even want to be thinking them. Everything about her life seemed to be up in the air as long as she had a wand up her sleeve and Lyndame was still out to get her. "I'm fine with avocados," she said at last.

"Well, that's settled, then," Sara said. "We can go home."

The pixies protested loudly at that. Calling out for hearings with the queen about working conditions and dietary requirements.

But something else was bothering Mira. *She* was the one who had played with Hipple so many times when she was small. And it was *her* mother who'd created the specifications for Fairy Village, Mira was sure. Maybe her mother had had a special connection with the pixies. Maybe Mira had a special connection too. Maybe here with the pixies was a place Mira could be safe from Lyndame, hidden by the magical pixie dust. Mira turned to Hipple. "Had you meant to come for me? You meant to find me and found Beans instead . . . isn't that right?"

Hipple shuffled, looking uncomfortable. A confused silence fell over the pixies.

"What're you talking about?" Sara said. "Everybody knows pixies only want to kidnap little kids for their queens."

"You don't know that," Mira said. "You didn't even know about the pixie dust. I'm the one who knew about it. I'm the pixie expert."

"Thee is too large to be our queen," Hipple interrupted. "Thee is *very* large."

"*I'm* the queen," Beans said.

"Long live the queen," the pixies said.

"May she ever grace our presence," the pixies said.

"Stop saying that!" Mira said.

"Why do you keep trying to leave?" Sara said to Mira, her

132

cheeks red. "Did you know Mom thinks those people kidnapped you? She called the police, but they said everything checked out. She didn't believe them. She didn't go to work so she could go out and look for you. I told her don't bother. I told her you wanted to go. That you went on purpose!"

What could Mira say? She *had* gone and gladly. "You wouldn't understand."

"You're right, I wouldn't," Sara said. "Don't you think we miss Papa too? Don't you know how special it is to have an actual family and live in an actual house? We're sad he's gone, but we're still a family. You should appreciate it a little more."

The use of the endearment "Papa" grated on Mira's nerves again. He was *her* Papa, and no one could miss him as much as she did. Plus, Mira *didn't* have a family. Or a house. The house belonged to Val now. "You don't know what you're talking about," Mira said.

Sara's lips pressed into a thin line.

Someone called in the distance. "Sara! Beans!" It was Mrs. Sutter.

"She's noticed you're gone," Mira said. "You need to go back, take Beans with you."

"What are you going to do?" Sara said.

"I need to put this wand where Lyndame can't get it. Can't use it to hurt me." As soon as Mira said that, an idea occurred to her. What better place to get rid of it than Glass Pond? She could throw it in. Sure, she could. She couldn't use it herself . . . surely not. But Lyndame *must* have come from there. If Mira threw the

133

wand into the pond, it would be back where it came from and Lyndame wouldn't be able to use it against her.

"Lyndame is the bad and dangerous person you told me about? Who is she?"

"Ah, well, she's my . . . aunt."

Sara's eyes bugged out. "An aunt who is trying to hurt you? Why? Is she from Glass Pond like your mom?"

The questions were overwhelming. Why *would* Lyndame want to hurt a member of her family? Why would she want to hurt Mira? What did it all have to do with her mom? Without thinking, Mira touched her sleeve, feeling the weight of the wand. "Never mind. I can't think about all that right now. And she's probably lying about being my aunt. She lies about everything. Just take Beans home."

Mrs. Sutter's calls were louder.

"But I don't understand," Sara said.

"I don't really either," Mira said. "But you and Beans have got to go."

"The queen cannot leave!" Hipple said.

The pixies began murmuring in their own language.

Mira, Sara, and Beans needed to be away before the pixies decided to do something to stop them, Mira realized. She wasn't sure *what* the pixies could do. "Come on!" she said to Beans.

"No, Mira!" Beans said. "I'm the queen of the pixies. I have to be with the pixies."

Once Beans set her mind to something, she could be super stubborn about changing it. But maybe she didn't have to.

Maybe she could be the queen and go home at the same time. Beans could take the pixies home with her, at least for now. That meant Mira needed to encourage the pixies to go to their house.

"You know," Mira said. "Queens make sure their subjects are provided for. My Barbie and Bratz clothes are in a bin in my attic. I'll bet the pixies would like some of those clothes. Gammy made these gorgeous dresses and suits, like with silk and lace and sequins."

The pixies stopped arguing. Their gazes focused her way.

"Do you think your subjects would like those clothes?" Mira continued, keeping her eyes on Beans. "You would just need to go home and get them."

The pixies looked at Beans hopefully.

Beans paused dramatically, then nobly said, "Okay."

The pixies cheered.

Mira made sure Sara and Beans were out of the cellar and on their way back home before she took off running toward Glass Pond.

Chapter Twenty-One

The entry chime sounded as Mira walked into Between
Grocery.

Miss Liu was there, talking to a woman behind the
counter. The woman had gray pigtails, medium-brown skin, tattoo sleeves, and red suspenders with jeans. She looked vaguely
familiar, so Mira assumed she must be Mrs. Martha.

The two women turned when Mira entered.

"What are you doing here?" Mira said to Miss Liu.

"I do have a life outside the library, Mira," Miss Liu said
with a smirk. "I'm here for lunch, naturally. Ahead of the crowd,
since I'm cleverer than most. The rest of Between will be along
shortly." She and Mrs. Martha laughed. Mira could see that Miss
Liu held a to-go container.

"Awfully young to be coming in here by yourself, aren't you?"
Mrs. Martha said to Mira.

"Mira is very independent," Miss Liu said. "She babysits for
her sisters all the time at the library."

"I remember you, child," Mrs. Martha said. "You used to

come in here with your father, didn't you? I was so sorry to hear about his passing. I've never seen anyone so fond of their little one as your father was about you."

Mira stopped still. She felt she might cry. Most people avoided talking about Papa, averted their eyes when the subject came up. But here was someone talking about the terrible day straight up, without being prompted. And it was true, what Mrs. Martha said. Papa had loved her so very much. No one would ever love Mira again as Papa had.

Miss Liu seemed to notice Mira's reaction. She strode over and took Mira's shoulder in a side hug. "She's doing quite well, aren't you, Mira? I've also noticed she and her sisters are very good readers. How's your grandchild, Mrs. Martha?"

Mrs. Martha launched into details about her grandson and something about a drawing that was hung in the lobby of the elementary school.

Mira tuned the conversation out, waiting, and it was only when a lull in the talking came that she blurted, "I need to get to Glass Pond. How do I get inside the gate?"

She had startled them, she could tell. They exchanged glances.

"That gate is locked, child," Mrs. Martha said. "There's no going in."

"Why would you think you needed to go there?" Miss Liu added.

They both frowned at her. Mira realized that she wasn't

going to get any information from them. So, she improvised. "It's . . . hot. I wanted to go for a swim."

"I see," Mrs. Martha said, obviously relieved. "It's too bad it's such a mucky pond. You wouldn't want to swim in there if you saw it. Full of algae and mosquitoes and water moccasins. Truly a mess. Be glad it's locked up tight."

"Yes," Miss Liu said. "But this spring *is* a scorcher. Why don't we talk to Mrs. Blaise about you and Sara and Beans coming to swim at my apartment complex pool sometime?"

Mira noticed Miss Liu carefully avoided calling Val "your mom." Mira had corrected Miss Liu on that months ago. Mira was always quick to correct people on that. And it was nice of Miss Liu to offer her pool. On a regular day Mira might have been excited about the prospect. But today was not a regular day. "That would be nice . . . sometime," Mira said. "Anyway, I've got to be going. Lots to do today."

"I see. Well, I hope to see you at the library soon," Miss Liu said.

"Pool toys are on sale on the back wall," Mrs. Martha said. "You should check them out."

"Okay," Mira said, and wandered over to stare at inflatables and diving toys, although she wasn't really looking at them. She was wondering how she was going to get through the gate to the pond. There was no lock to pick, not that she knew how to pick locks. She could hack through the wood with a chainsaw, she supposed, except she didn't have a chainsaw. An extra-tall ladder might be good for getting over the fence, but she didn't have one of those either. Climbing the fence was the only option she could think of. She'd just have to try it.

She was starting to head out when she noticed that Miss Liu and Mrs. Martha had lowered their voices and were whispering. So, instead of leaving, Mira ducked down behind an aisle and crept closer to the counter to listen.

". . . secret must be protected . . ."

". . . it's not as if it would work for her . . ."

Mira's stomach churned; she felt certain they were talking about her.

Someone tapped her on the shoulder from behind and she squelched a yelp.

The ancient woman in the turquoise dress, also crouched. It was the woman who had followed Mira the day before. The woman inclined her head toward the door. *Come with me,* she meant. She slipped soundlessly down the aisle.

Mira soon followed. "Bye! Thank you!" she called innocently as the chime sounded.

She hurried around to the back of the building, where she felt sure the ancient woman would be waiting for her, and nearly ran smack into . . .

Mrs. Martha, who must've gone out a back door. Out from behind the counter, the woman was taller than Mira had realized.

"Lost your way?" Mrs. Martha said. She eyed Mira's trajectory toward Glass Pond and arched a brow.

"I was just looking for . . . you know, the frogs," Mira said.

"The frogs," Mrs. Martha repeated.

"Yes," Mira said. "I collect them and put them in jars with holes in the lids. I thought there might be some near the, um, water."

"Where's your jar, then?"

"Jar?"

Mrs. Martha's eyes narrowed. "To put the frogs in."

"Oh, you're right! I've forgotten it. I'll just run home and get one."

"There aren't any frogs here, child. I suggest you look elsewhere."

"Are you sure? I mean . . ."

"Nope, no frogs. Not a one. Head on home now, dear." Mrs. Martha folded her arms across her chest and set her eyes on Mira until Mira, quite intimidated, laughed awkwardly, backed up, and headed around the building toward the parking lot.

Miss Liu was still in the lot. She waved at Mira from the driver's window of her car; she seemed to be waiting for Mira to clear out before she left.

Mira kept walking, feeling Miss Liu's eyes on her back. When she reached the I-78 crosswalk and looked back, Miss Liu was still watching from her car. And Mrs. Martha had come around to the front of the building, her gaze also locked on Mira. The teenager with the curly hair, the one she'd talked to the day before, had cycled up to the grocery, and even *he* was turned around, straddling his bike, eyes on Mira.

All three of them watched her until she crossed the highway and was well on her way toward home.

*** *

It took forever for Mira to double back, or at least it felt like it. The only crosswalk over I-78 was in front of the gas station and grocery, which Mrs. Martha might be guarding. So, Mira ended up down the street, forcing her way through the brush of a heavily wooded section in order to cross I-78 at a mad dash with *no crosswalk*.

But finally, she was sneaking along the length of the black-painted fence toward the path to the gate.

The woman in turquoise was sitting cross-legged in front of a hydrangea bush, waiting. When she saw Mira, she sprang up without a word and scurried down the path. The woman moved fast for someone so old, her leafy dress fluttering behind her.

"Wait!" Mira said, and hurried to catch up.

When they met at the gate, the woman began talking rapid-fire in that other language, gesturing at the gate.

"Yes, I want inside," Mira said. "Do you know how to get in?"

The woman held her wrinkled palm inches from the worn iron plate mounted on the gate; the plate that was in the spot where a handle should have been. She waggled her woody eyebrows. Then she pointed at Mira's hand.

"You want me to put my hand there?" Mira said. "Like this?" And she held her palm inches from the iron plate, exactly as the woman had done.

The woman pushed Mira's hand against the plate.

A puff of sparks. A humanlike sound, *Ahhh*, that seemed to come from the gate itself.

141

With a cry, Mira yanked her hand away. Not that it'd hurt. She felt nothing but cold metal.

The gate clicked and swung open.

"Was that a fingerprint scanner or something? What was that sound? Why did my hand work?" Mira said, a bit breathless.

The woman nodded unhelpfully and then skipped back down the path.

Mira paused only a moment before she walked inside, leaving the gate open behind her. It didn't occur to her to close it. Although based on what happened after, she probably should have.

The path inside the gate wound between loblolly pines and sweetgum trees. A slow and sultry wind smelling of cooking meat and spices stirred the leaves above her.

When Mira arrived at the pond, she found it wasn't quite as mucky as Mrs. Martha had described. In fact, the pond wasn't mucky at all. It was a pretty pond—glimmering and still, surrounded by delicate ferns and stalwart cattails and garlanded by waterlilies blooming with lilac flowers. And it was much smaller than Mira had expected, given all the rumors it inspired. It was no more than twelve feet across.

Mira fingered the lace cuff of her sleeve, not quite touching the wand. She would just throw it into the water, any minute now. But where would it go? She couldn't tell how deep the pond was; the surface reflected the sky and she couldn't see into the water. Now that she was actually there, she wondered . . . if she threw it in, would the wand merely sink a few feet and be easy for Lyndame to retrieve?

Wouldn't it be better and safer, Mira thought, to keep the wand for herself? She wouldn't use it, except maybe for her own defense.

Or for finding her grandmother.

Mira realized with a start of surprise that she'd been considering this possibility since the moment the wand came into her hand. Because if Lyndame had come up out of the pond, as Mira suspected, didn't that mean her grandmother was from there too? Somehow down inside the water . . .

As Mira studied the surface, wondering what she should do, a figure appeared next to her reflection, just over her shoulder. A small figure, standing on a cloud, or so it seemed, waving at her. She glanced up at the sky. No small figure there. Nothing but clouds. But on the surface of the pond, she could swear she saw it.

She knelt at the water's edge, the knees of her jeans quickly becoming soaked in the damp earth, to look closer. It was very tiny. But was that . . . Papa? Yes, the figure might be wearing gray coveralls, like Papa had worn to work, and could that be a tiny smudge of red at the pocket, where Papa's coveralls had read *CHARLES*? The figure waved harder.

"Are you trying to tell me something?" Mira said to the reflection.

The figure kept waving.

"Do I have a grandmother in there? Would she love me like Gammy did?" Mira said.

"Mira!" someone shouted. It was Val, on the path, hurrying her way. Val wore a khaki trench coat and lime-colored gardening boots over flowered pajamas. It was a bizarre outfit. Why was she dressed like that? "That boy in the grocery told me you were asking about the pond," Val called. "I need to know what's going on here—Don't do it!"

What did Val think Mira was doing? What *was* Mira doing? She stood. Because she suddenly *knew* what she was doing. And it wasn't throwing the wand away. Far from it.

"It's okay!" Mira called.

"No!" Val said.

Before Val could reach her, Mira quickly waded into the pond. The slope was steeper than she'd expected; the water got deep fast.

The water was also cold, which was odd for this time of year.

That was her last thought before the water reached up and pulled her under.

Chapter Twenty-Two

Mira emerged in a dimly lit place, gasping for air and clinging to a grimy metal chain, her body numb from the cold. She hauled herself out onto what felt like a rough wooden dock, one leg at a time, and then she collapsed, a searing pain in her chest as she hacked up water.

She was no longer at Glass Pond in Between, that was clear.

"Mackes fillid," someone said in an annoyed-sounding voice. She could have sworn it meant something like, *Move along, idiot.*

She struggled to sit up, to get out of the way.

It wasn't a dock. It was a wooden catwalk. There were many of the catwalks, going this way and that, over the glassy surface of a lake. A lake that reflected the buildings encircling it, castle-like buildings with towers and parapets. In the reddened sky were a dozen globes like small suns. The smells were like that of a circus: sweat and cooking meat and the foulest waste. But it was like no circus Mira had ever seen.

There were people, a great many, but also *creatures*. Creatures who traveled the catwalks, emerged from the water, jumped in. A feathery mound with jutting teeth and taloned feet. A troll with ram-like horns and a wriggling sack over its shoulder. A shrouded figure with arms that branched into multiple hands and a heavily jeweled crown, a pack on its back.

Fairy-tale creatures from Mira's worst nightmares, all crowded into one location. All with someplace to be, or so it seemed.

And what was even worse? The place was *huge*. How was she supposed to find her grandmother here?

"Oh no," Mira whispered. She could have cried right about then. Or at the very least, curled up into a ball and pretended she was back home. She must be dreaming, she had to be, but it certainly *felt* real. Her toes were cold in the sloshy (but still glittery) sneakers, water clogged her left ear like it often did after swimming, and her hand stung where she'd scraped it on the catwalk climbing out of the water.

Yes, she could be dreaming, she supposed, but if she was dreaming, would she be supposing about it? Or would she not even be thinking about the possibility that she was dreaming?

She got to her feet, water streaming everywhere, and addressed a small girl in a long white dress who was walking by. "Excuse me. What is this place?"

"Speak the common tongue!" the girl roared in a deep baritone, her jaw unhinging.

Startled, Mira tripped backward and nearly fell off the catwalk, her flailing hand catching a post at the last moment.

The small girl kept going, unbothered.

Mira shook her head, trying to clear it. Her brain felt as waterlogged as her shoes. What was *that*? It was clear that things weren't always what they seemed here. But where was *here*? She had to find out.

"Obviously, you are in One-Place-or-the-Other" was the sort of answer Mira got, or "Fillid," which, from the way it was said, did seem to mean something like *idiot*. No one seemed to understand what she was asking, or they simply weren't interested in answering. One tiny creature's response was to launch at her with its teeth, and Mira was happy she was wearing the glittery sneakers, and particularly glad they were high-tops. She took a few turns and soon lost her bearings; she couldn't have said where she emerged from the water.

Right after Mira's latest inquiry was ignored by a many-tongued creature with no eyes, she quite by accident came to a place where the catwalk connected to the land, and she stepped off onto a shadowy avenue with pavers that made it look like a honeycomb. From that vantage, she could see that the buildings surrounding the lake were all of a piece, a continuous, strangely designed structure, with haphazard additions and tunnel-like alleys, the entire construction doughnut-shaped.

Everyone (and everything!) walked on the avenue. There were no vehicles, scooters, or bikes; there wouldn't have been space for them. Along the building, the throngs of people and creatures were denser, the smells stronger. The occasional lingerer cooked over small fires in various nooks, counted what looked like pebbles, or glared out from the tunnels. There were no directional signs, anything that looked like lettering, or even helpful arrows of any sort.

Mira's steps grew slower and slower until she stopped, uncertain of where to go next.

A tall, spindly creature peered down at her as it passed, abruptly collapsing in height until its lizard-like eyes met hers. The scaly skin was rippling and rearranging, the creature's appearance transforming until it looked like, well, it looked like *her*, another Mira. A small, scared, and thoroughly wet-looking Mira. A Mira who *winked* at her. Then the creature changed again, stretching up into its tall, thin self. It continued on without having broken its stride.

"What—" Mira sputtered.

"Paper flower for your hair?" a man asked her. "Impervious to water. I've got them in every color." He had an armful of paper flowers, and perhaps to demonstrate, he was wearing dozens in his hair. They were—every single one of them—the same shade of brown.

"Ah, no thank you," Mira said, and, realizing he was speaking English, added, "Can you tell me where I am?" But the man had already moved on, making his offer to a giant hedgehog wearing a crown.

It was amazing, to be sure, but Mira's head spun at being in such a strange place, and what's more, she was cold. The suns or lights in the sky, or whatever they were, were too far away to bring much warmth to the shadows against the building. She took off her cropped vest, which was soaked, and carried it, hoping her shirt would dry, shivering as she walked.

It occurred to her for the first time that she didn't know how to get back to Between. It was a frightening thought.

"Please," Mira said to a woman with a veil over her face. "Can you tell me where I am?"

The woman's head tilted and her eyes gleamed through the veil. "My dear, I heard you ask that gentleman the same question. I believe you must be confused. You are in One-Place-or-the-Other, the *between* place, the Waystation. There are pleasures to be had here, to be sure, and bartering to be done. But no one comes *here* unless they already know where they are going, their final destination, if you will."

Mira laughed nervously. "Right. Um, how do I find out where to go? Is there, like, a map somewhere?"

"Ah, I could show you some . . . maps. Behind one of the doors, perhaps." A glimpse, through the veil, of a movement around the woman's mouth. A flicker of a tongue, the flash of pointed teeth.

Even if Mira hadn't seen the teeth, she would have known, thanks to Val's lectures and Mira's own common sense, not to go behind a door with a stranger. "No thanks. I was confused. I've just remembered where I'm going." She hurried away from the woman (or whatever she was), taking her great disappointment with her.

Mira had assumed that she would go directly to her grand-mother, somehow. But she now saw how foolish that assumption had been. Even if this place worked like a train station, Mira was only *partway* there. And she didn't know where her grandmother lived or how to make her way there even if she were to find out. How was Mira going to find her?

What *did* she know?

Well, she knew her mother's name had been Aisling. She knew her mother had owned an emerald-green pendant that apparently was an amulet. Mira had the vague impression an amulet was used as protection, was meant to ward off bad things, but in any case, it was an amulet that Mira *no longer had*. She also knew Lyndame's name, if "Lyndame" was even a real name.

It didn't add up to much.

Mira was getting a headache. "Excuse me," she said to a man with a blue beard. "Do you know a human-type person who had a daughter named Aisling?"

The man's whole head swiveled in her direction, and bulbous eyes latched onto hers. Maybe she shouldn't have tried this one. He was a good seven feet tall. "Where is this person from?" his voice boomed.

"Um, I don't know."

"Well, what do they look like?"

"I don't know that either."

The man had a barking laugh. "This will be a joke, then, eh? A good one, I'm sure!" He clapped a hand down on Mira's shoulder, knocking her to her knees.

Other people and creatures seemed to laugh with him, or to make noises to each other that Mira interpreted as laughter. Her face warmed to her hairline.

Mira was having a bad day. Not only had the parents of her dreams vanished into nothingness, but she'd nearly drowned getting to a strange and creepy place with no notion of how to get home, and now ridiculous-looking creatures were laughing at her. On top of that, she was cold and hungry, having had nothing to eat since breakfast. To say that she'd reached the end of her rope would be . . . well, about right, really.

"That's it!" Mira fumbled clumsily with her sleeve while a small audience watched. The man with the blue beard had moved on, but a goblin, a man with a wolf's head, and a boy in tattered clothes were paying attention.

"I've been so polite, this whole time"—and here Mira withdrew the wand in all its glittering glory—"but now I want to know: Where. Is. My. Grandmother?" She waved the wand around while she spoke, and it *did* have the effect she wanted. Or possibly, she overshot.

She was alone in a large swath of avenue. Creatures shoved each other in attempts to get even farther away. No more chattering, no more grunts or snarls. The air was filled only with the clanging of the wand. And it shone brilliantly in this dim place, making it clear the wand had never been reflecting sunlight; it was the *source* of the light.

"Put that away, fillid!" someone shouted.

"Who said that?" Mira said. "Why should I?"

The boy in tattered clothes. He stood in the shadows by the building, the only individual remaining within twenty feet. "Put it away and I'll tell you," he said.

Since he seemed to be the only one likely to tell her much of anything, she did as he asked.

He stepped into the light. Black curly hair, light brown skin. He appeared to be a standard sort of boy. Though it was likely, Mira thought, that his jaw could come unhinged or he had sharp teeth or some other hidden feature. "Come on," he said.

"I'm not going anywhere with you."

"We're not going anywhere. We just need to walk. You need to *look* like you're going somewhere in this place or you'll get knocked in the head. Trust me on this."

"I don't know who you are."

"I'm Tomas," he said. "So now you know."

She fell into step beside him. A minotaur hulking over a fire watched them pass.

"Second mistake you've made," Tomas said. "You can't trust anyone here. Not a soul will aid you."

Mira snorted. "Aren't you helping me?"

"Not at all. I'm simply telling you not to use the wand while you're in One-Place-or-the-Other. Keep it to yourself. You can't use weapons here. They're illegal. I won't report you, but someone will. You'll be locked up and disallowed from the Middleway."

"The Middleway?"

"The water. The Middleway. Do you know nothing? How'd you get here?"

Mira stifled her annoyance. Tomas was giving her more information than she'd gotten all day. "I jumped into a pond back home."

Tomas sighed. "Yes, as you've found, if you don't have a destination in mind when you enter the Middleway, you'll end up here. You're from the land of highways, yes? You should return there. Highway-land people tend to get lost out here."

Georgia *did* have a lot of highways. Mira supposed that was what he meant. "I can't. I'm looking for my grandmother. Except I don't know how to find her."

"I can't help you with that. But if you discover the name of her location, you can use the Middleway to get there. You must keep your destination firmly in mind when you jump; otherwise you'll only end up back here, or someplace unexpected. It helps to state the name aloud right before. Then once you've found her, you can go back home. You *should* go back home."

"I just say the name?"

"While keeping it firmly in your mind, yes. And don't be so foolish as to wave that wand around again. The moment you use it, they'll be on you."

Tomas grabbed hold of a ladder and scrambled up.

"Wait!" Mira called.

But Tomas was a fast climber. He was nearly to a door. "Goodly travels!" he called.

Tomas had accused her of being foolish, but he *had* told her how to travel the Middleway, which was significantly more than she'd known moments before. "Thank you!" Mira called.

She now knew how to get back to Between. But she was not going back to Between. She had to find her grandmother. She had to.

"Help!" someone shouted from the water.

Mira recognized the voice. It was Sara.

Chapter Twenty-Three

S ara, *what* are you doing?" Mira shouted. "Swim to the side!"

Sara was out in the Middleway, in the water, holding on to a partly submerged catwalk, like a shipwreck survivor holds on to an overturned ship, her blond head just above the surface.

"I can't! I'm stuck!" Sara's voice echoed over the water.

Of course she was stuck. But why was she even here? Why did Sara always have to poke her nose into whatever Mira was doing?

The submerged section of catwalk was turned on its side. Mira squinted at it. Overturned like that, it kind of looked like . . . well, it sort of looked like a balance beam. Fine. Mira was great at balance beam. She could walk out and release Sara. After that, Mira could go on to find her grandmother. She took a deep breath. "I'm coming!"

"Don't, it's dangerous!" Sara said.

The catwalk did look as if it was about to sink into the water. When Mira stepped on it, it sank a little more, but it was still connected to the other catwalks and seemed to be holding, at least for the moment. She put out her arms to steady herself. Near her feet, rows of red gelatinous creatures attached to the catwalk's underside were exposed, and they wriggled as she walked along, tiny mouths opening and closing, as if they were trying to tell her something.

The noise coming from the avenue increased. An audience had gathered and its members babbled intensely. A glance behind revealed they were passing handfuls of stones back and forth. They were *betting*, Mira suspected. Maybe on how fast she could make it back or if she'd fall into the water and drown.

"Cut that out!" Mira said.

"Mira, it's mad about the catwalk overturning. Be careful!" Sara said.

It?

In the water, a dark shape the size of a city bus swept by Mira. A flat black eye regarded her.

Uh-oh.

"I'm scared," Sara said.

Mira made her voice tough. "Things are never as scary as they are in your head." Papa had always said that.

"It's not in my head. It's right there!"

Well, that was true, Mira thought. Her heart was beating a staccato—she was scared too. What she needed was the wand. Tomas had warned her not to use it, but this was an emergency. She tried to reach for it and nearly lost her balance, windmilling her arms. She would get closer to Sara before she took it out,

156

she decided. She quickened her pace, trying to walk with light steps. It would've been easier if she wasn't wearing soggy sneakers. "How are you stuck?" Mira said.

"My foot, it's wedged in the boards. I was trying to get out of the water, and the catwalk broke. It's all rotted. I didn't mean for it to flip."

Leave it to Sara to break the catwalk.

The dark shape was circling back around.

A few feet before she reached Sara, Mira stopped; the part of the catwalk that Sara was clinging to was mostly underwater. "Don't talk," Mira said.

Sara ignored that. "How're you going to get me out?"

Mira bit her lip. There was no time to swim underneath and unwedge Sara's foot. The dark shape was swimming back. A glimpse of a slimy red arm with suckers the size of dinner plates. It was some sort of squid. "I said don't talk!"

The squid monster was getting nearer. Coming toward Mira.

Mira took the wand from her sleeve, and a blazing light poured out onto the Middleway, silvering the greenish water and thrumming the air.

The laughing and talking at the shoreline ceased. The crowd was impressed.

The squid monster was not. It sped up, almost to Mira.

What to do? What had Lyndame said about the wand? About how she used it? Something about visualizing . . .

The massive squid rose up, tentacles slipping around the

catwalk at Mira's feet, a huge, beaked mouth gaping open.

Mira launched into the ugliest and most desperate side flip ever known to man. Or girl. Her squad-mates would have been mortified on her behalf.

Immediately after she did, the mouth crunched down on the catwalk where she'd been standing.

No way for Mira to land the flip. The catwalk wasn't beneath her anymore.

A rush of dark and cold.

She was in the water.

Bubbles, large red arms, and tentacles were everywhere. She swam hard to reach the surface, panic seizing her. She'd lost the wand!

She burst out of the water, gasping for air. *Where* was Sara? She wasn't where she'd been a moment before. The catwalk either. The squid monster's attack must've made Sara's section sink further. Mira had to free her. But how? And how far under had Sara been pulled?

Mira swam desperately toward the spot where she'd last seen Sara—or at least she hoped it was the spot—forgetting everything she'd learned from swimming lessons; she splashed frantically as the squid monster roiled the waters around her.

Mira imagined the catwalk sinking, sinking, sinking, Sara twenty feet down, now thirty, now one hundred feet, that blond head and yellow T-shirt being pulled into the murky depths by the foot still hopelessly wedged into the catwalk's boards.

But then . . . Was that . . . Oh yes! The sparkle of the wand, *in Sara's hand*, sticking up from the water and waving at her. And Mira's imaginings were wrong because Sara had clearly been pulled just below the surface, not far down at all. She had somehow caught the wand, and even though her head was now under and she was surely panicked too, she held it out for Mira.

The moment Mira wrapped her fingers around the wand, a giant tentacle wrapped around her leg. The wand thrummed to life. She waved it and visualized as hard as she could. "Out!" she said.

The sound of bells. The word *OUT* sparkling gold and silver in the sky like a fireworks display. And a tremendous belching. The Middleway ejecting her. And there she was, soaring.

No, not her alone. A shining mass of squid monster soared through the air with her. She hadn't visualized *that*. But oh yes, a spot of yellow too. That Zoo Atlanta T-shirt. Sara.

The wand had worked for Mira.

It had wooooorrrrrkkkkkkeeeed.

Mira landed on a hellhound, hard. "Sorry!" she said. The hound yipped in pain and fled, knocking her to the pavers, where she fell onto her hands, the wand slipping back into her sleeve.

Others in the crowd weren't as lucky as the hound. A whole host was buried beneath the glistening mass of squid monster. Onlookers shouted as the monster desperately tried to get back into the water, arms flailing.

"Let her go!" Sara was shouting from somewhere. "She just wants her babies!"

"Babies?" Mira said, scrambling to her feet as Sara appeared.

159

"They were under the catwalk—the same color. Didn't you see?" Sara said. "Egg sac–looking things. She's a mom, I think. That's why she attacked. She's protecting them. Maybe they shouldn't have been out of the water."

Mira hadn't wondered *why* the monster had attacked. But the mention of *mom* made her want to know . . . "Where's *your* mom? Why are you here? Why aren't you at home? Why didn't you go back to Mrs. Sutter?"

A tremendous splash and a surge of water over the avenue as the squid monster returned to the Middleway. A loud cracking as the section of catwalk broke off the rest of the way.

"The babies are in the water now. That's good." Sara then turned to Mira. "I told Beans to go back to Mrs. Sutter, and then, well, I followed you to Glass Pond. When I saw you and Mom jump in, I jumped in too."

"I remember Val was behind me . . . She went in the pond too?" *Why* had Val done that? She was just making everything more complicated.

"Yup. Mom went after you. She must be here somewhere."

"This is a disaster," Mira said.

"By the way, I helped you. Did you notice?" Sara's smile was ghastly—she'd cut her lip, and her teeth were smeared with blood. "You needed my help. If I hadn't caught the wand, we'd be squid food. I helped you. You needed me."

"That's true. I did need your help. You did good." Something else occurred to Mira. "You got the pouch away from Hipple too. You've got good hands."

"Yes! I should play softball. Shortstop, for sure. Or I could be a famous football receiver. How'd you use that wand anyway? Can I get one?"

The wand was back in Mira's sleeve, although she didn't remember putting it there. "No, you can't have one and I shouldn't have used it either. I heard it's not—"

Crack!

A dazzling light and three figures appeared out of nowhere, bent over Mira and Sara. The figures were elegant, wondrous, and fearsome: eight feet tall with cascading white hair, horns like corkscrews, and pointed hats; daggers hung at the waists of their robes of green, violet, and blue, respectively.

Wizards, is what they looked like.

Mira squeaked in fear.

"Cool," Sara breathed.

"Twaken!" the wizards said in unison. They went on, speaking in that other language, their thundering voices seeming to come from everywhere at once. The blue wizard twirled a ball of light menacingly. An audience had formed to witness whatever horrible thing was about to happen to Mira. The wizards *seemed* to be scolding her, although she couldn't be positive . . .

"I don't understand you," Mira said, her voice small.

The wizards switched to English. "Weapons!" they said. "Are not allowed here!"

"Um, it was an accident," Mira said. "See, there was this squid monster upset about her babies . . ."

Someone tittered.

161

"She made a mess of the Middleway!" said a shepherd with a staff. "And just look at what she done to Bernard." The hellhound lowered his red eyes and whimpered.

"You are fine, you big wimp," Sara said.

"Let me through! Those are my kids!" It was Val, shouting from somewhere.

The blue wizard held the ball of light closer to Mira.

Inside her sleeve, the wand quivered. Mira could feel it twitching more and more violently, until it abruptly shot out of her cuff to slam against the ball of light like a pin sticking to a magnet.

"A Wand of Wynfarish," the blue wizard declared.

"Wynfarish?" Mira said.

"Remanded to jail," the other wizards said. "At once."

"Uh-oh," Sara said.

A wizard grabbed Mira by the arm. The long white fingers pinched. They were taking her somewhere.

Crack!

162

Chapter Twenty-Four

Mira was behind bars. The metal cage was the size of her family room, although nowhere near as pleasant. There was plenty of evidence others had been there before her: foul-smelling stains, clumps of brownish hair collected in the corners, a yellowed, bone-like object as long as her finger that looked suspiciously like a tooth.

It was an ogre jail. Or more specifically, the ogres were the guards. Six feet tall and nearly that big around, the gray-green ogres had heads like boulders and huge, muscled arms that extended past their relatively small legs to brush the ground. Their navy coveralls put Mira in mind of hoop tents.

In the few hours Mira had been in the jail, it had become clear that the ogres' favorite activity was darts. Two ogres lounged in rough-hewn chairs while they leisurely tossed the darts through the cage to the wooden wall on the other side. A third ogre, the smallest, had to retrieve the darts for the bigger two. He ran around and around the cage, constantly tripping on his too-long coveralls and becoming as sweaty as Mira.

Mira was sweaty because she was dashing back and forth,

dodging the darts, which were the size of arrows and appeared awfully sharp. Although the ogres didn't seem to actually want to hit her as much as they enjoyed her terrified running. "When are you going to let me go?" she asked, breathless.

"Eight days to Sunday," the first ogre said.

"Three days after forever," the second ogre said.

They chortled, slapping each other's shoulders.

"Who's your next of kin, little girl?" the first ogre asked.

"Why do you need that? Isn't that who you notify when someone dies?" Mira said.

The ogres laughed even harder.

Did she have a next of kin? Mira wondered. Val was in One-Place-or-the-Other; Mira had heard Val shouting just before the wizards had taken her here. But of course, Mira and Val weren't related. Val probably only came to satisfy herself that New Mom and New Dad hadn't been legit, as she'd suspected. She probably hadn't believed in them because she couldn't believe anyone would want Mira to begin with. No, Mira's next of kin was not Val. It was her grandmother, Mira decided, the one she hadn't met yet. The one she *needed* to meet.

At last, the ogres retired to their table to drink out of tankards the size of water buckets and eat entire roasts of turkey.

Mira collapsed against the cold bars, feeling sorry for herself. Her clothes hadn't dried from her adventures in the Middleway, and her jeans chafed. Her tangled hair hung in her face, and she had a blister on her toe from running back and forth in soggy sneakers.

The smallest ogre—his name was Hermit—leaned against the wall littered with dart holes. He breathed heavily, rings of sweat staining his coveralls. "Don't worry," he whispered. "They're not serious. You'll get a hearing with the wizards, I feel sure."

Mira sniffled and tucked a snarled lock of hair behind an ear. "When will that be?"

"Dunno," Hermit said. "Whenever they get the time, I guess. They're supposed to be back by quarter past thirteen o'clock, but we'll see."

"That's not very reassuring."

"They're not very reassuring, wizards," Hermit said. "They're not very nice."

Well, that was even less assuring.

The bigger ogres rose from the table, stretching and yawning. "You're in charge, Hermit! We'll be back after nap o'clock!" They laughed and tromped out a rear door.

When the door closed behind them, Hermit let out a long breath. He slid down the wall to land heavily on his rump. He wasn't too intimidating, that Hermit.

"Do you have a grandmother, Hermit? I'm on my way to see mine," Mira said.

"Captain Jara," he said. "You do not want to toy with her. She is one tough ogre." His eyes widened at the statement. Although he had matted hair, a jutting forehead, and a bulbous nose like the other two ogres, he had nice eyes, Mira thought. Forest-green irises and long lashes.

Mira supposed her grandmother might be tough. But somehow, she didn't think so. Mira imagined a white-haired woman gasping in delight when Mira appeared, dropping her crossword puzzle to leap up with open arms, ready to embrace her long-lost grandchild.

"What're you thinking of?" Hermit said. "It must be nice."

"I was imagining what my grandmother will be like."

"You've never met her?"

"No."

"Well, you'll meet mine. Captain Jara usually runs the hearings. She's out in the country now, though. Don't know when she'll be back."

That made it seem like it would be a long time before Mira got her hearing. She would have to figure out a way to escape before then. She eyed the bars; they looked rusty but solid. "Do you know of a place called Wynfarish? The blue wizard said my wand was a 'Wand of Wynfarish.'"

"Yes, that's where your wand is from, all right. Powerful wands, those."

"It's not mine, not really. I only got it from my aunt today. And I *had* to take it from her. She appeared in Between and, well, she tried to kill me with it."

"Criminal type, then. Those wands are illegal even in Wynfarish. Most likely it was stolen."

"Stolen?" Why was Mira surprised? She already knew Lyndame was a thief. "Who did she steal it from?"

"Dunno. Don't know much about Wynfarish. Only that

they don't allow the wands to be used anymore," Hermit said.

Lyndame had wanted Mira dead so badly she'd stolen a wand, then gone through an elaborate charade, pretending she could grant wishes. Why had she gone to so much trouble? What was Lyndame so angry about?

"Got into a pickle, haven't you?" Hermit said. "And not of your own making."

He sounded sympathetic, Mira thought. "That's right. I didn't steal it. And I only used it the once. Maybe you could let me out now that the others are gone."

He was already shaking his head before she finished making the suggestion. "Can't do it. My brothers would smash me to bits. Besides, you can't be using weapons in One-Place-or-the-Other. They make it unsafe here. You'll need a proper punishment or others will also try to break the rules." Hermit had a righteous tone to his voice. He was not going to let her out.

She sighed.

"There's no need for you to be miserable. Let me get you something to eat." Hermit rose to his feet with a groan and mutterings about his aching shins.

The wand glittered at Mira from the wall; it hung between a bloodstained hatchet and a double-edged sword. Even if Mira could get her hands on the wand, she couldn't use it to escape. The wizards would catch her if she tried to use it, she knew. But the wand was a connection between Mira and Wynfarish, where she surely needed to go. She might need it to convince her grandmother that she was who she said she was. For that reason, she needed to get it back, assuming she could figure out some other way to escape.

"Here you go," Hermit said, pushing a burlap sack between the bars. The sack contained wrinkled apples, soft carrots, and a hard brown loaf of bread, all of which looked to have been there a while.

Mira wasn't picky. She quickly started on an apple.

Hermit watched her. "Yes, you eat your fill. And like I said, don't worry. You'll most likely get a hearing. I'm sure the wizards will arrive before their quarter-past-thirteen-o'clock deadline, and you won't be eaten."

Mira nearly choked on the apple. "Eaten?"

"Well, sure. It's why the ogres agreed to run the jail in the first place. What would be in it for us otherwise? But, like I said, don't worry, we only get to eat maybe half the inmates."

Mira forced the bite down her throat, swallowing hard. "You *eat* half the inmates?"

"Give or take. No worries, though. It doesn't hurt to get eaten 'cause we club you good first."

Mira dropped the bag. She had lost her appetite. She moved to the center of the cage, away from the kindly smile of Hermit, and sinking into a seated position, she made herself as small as possible—pulling her legs in close and putting her chin on her knees.

Other items in the jail took on a worrying significance: the open hearth in the corner, full of soot, a crane across the top supporting iron pots of varying sizes. The surface of the large table, stained dark, scattered bones on the floor beneath. The section of wall with hanging tools like cleavers and knives; maybe those tools weren't confiscated weapons like the rest.

It was drafty in the jail. She started to shiver.

"Would you like a blanket?" Hermit said.

"No, I'm good," Mira said.

When was thirteen o'clock? Or was that just another one of the ogres' nonsense sayings? It could mean anytime now, for all Mira knew.

How would the ogres eat her? she wondered. Would they tear her to pieces first or would they gnaw on her whole like the roasted turkeys? And had those actually *been* roasted turkeys in the first place?

She pictured herself reduced to a few discarded bones under the table, unidentifiable, the bones turning into the tiniest shards as the ogres stamped over them day after day. No one would ever know she was here, looking for her grandmother.

Meeting her grandmother was starting to seem impossible. Really, her odds of even surviving One-Place-or-the-Other were not looking good.

* * *

Mira's cheek was pressed into the cold metal floor of the cage, and she lay in a puddle of her own drool. She didn't know how long she'd slept there. Maybe for a few hours?

Her shivering must've woken her.

Or maybe it was Hermit's loud snoring; he was slumped against the wall, closer to Mira than she'd prefer.

Or maybe it was the squeaking.

A group of mice were trying to get into the discarded bag of food. Up the bag, down, around. The bag had flopped closed. They couldn't get in. *Squeak, squeak.* Apparently, this endeavor required a lot of discussion. They gnawed on the burlap.

"Oh, here you go," Mira said, scooting over to open the bag.

They squeaked their thanks and dashed inside, filled their cheeks with bread, and then dashed out again, disappearing into a crevice in the far wall. Then they were back. They were clearly taking the food to their hiding place. Back and forth, back and forth. They left pelleted droppings in their wake, as mice do.

"Well, I'm definitely not eating that food now," Mira said to herself. Not that she'd planned to.

The mice seemed to be a family: a bigger one and five tiny ones that must be the babies. The little gray-furred family reminded her of the fox family, the one that had helped her. Too bad these mice were too small to help her escape. If they put on a threatening display, the ogres wouldn't even notice it. The mice also wouldn't be able to retrieve the key to unlock the cage. She'd seen it when the ogres first locked her in. The key was significantly bigger than all of the mice put together. Mira didn't know where the key was anyway. The larger ogres had it somewhere.

Mira blinked. She'd been distracted by her thoughts and hadn't noticed the bigger mouse come to stand right in front of her. It stood on its hind legs, pink nose quivering, gazing at her.

The littler mice had gone; they must've gathered what food they could.

The mouse seemed to be waiting for something.

"I don't have any more," Mira said, and showed her empty hands.

That apparently wasn't what it wanted. It kept gazing at her.

"Did you want to thank me, then?" Mira said. "You're welcome."

The mouse's head bobbed. Still, it didn't leave. Its nose quivered some more.

Mira studied it. "Oh, I see you're wondering about me. No, I don't want to be here." She came down to her elbows to look at the mouse.

It backed up but then stepped forward again, like it was interested in what she had to say.

"You know," she said. "I called out to the foxes, I think. Not on purpose. But I was calling out for someone. I needed help, and I said it exactly like that: 'Help me.' I'm not sure what you could do, but do you think there's a way you could help me to get out of here?"

It stared at her a beat longer, then scampered away.

She didn't know if it understood her or not.

But Mira wrapped her arms around herself and pinned all her hopes on the little mouse.

Chapter Twenty-Five

The wall of the ogres' jail exploded in an eruption of mortar and brick.

Mira screamed and tried to shield herself from the flying debris.

Hermit was running around shouting, "What is it? What is it?"

Mira wiped dust from her eyes.

It hadn't actually been an explosion. Something had knocked a hole into the wall from the outside. A something large that was emerging out of the hole and into the jail: a furry creature the size of a rhino, five feet high to the shoulder, with a huge head hung low and a pointed horn the length of a hockey stick.

No, it actually *was* a rhino, covered in shaggy yellowish hair—a woolly rhino. Mira had seen pictures of them in science class. They were extinct. Only . . . that one was right there.

And it had a passenger riding behind the hump on its back.

"Mira." *Miwa.* "It's taco night and I want avamacados." Beans was wearing her crown—and a regal expression on her incredibly dirty face.

"The queen is in need of avamacados," a pixie said from

somewhere. "Thee must provide them."

"Beans?!" Mira said. "What are *you* doing here?"

"Having fun," Beans said. "Making friends."

A glimpse of a blond head, a figure slipping in through the hole in the wall. "See the cage there, Claude," Sara said. "Can you break it?"

The rhino screamed like a wild boar and pawed the ground with a front hoof. Mira had barely enough time to scramble to a far corner of the cage before the charging rhino left the barred door mangled and dangling from a single hinge.

"No, you can't do this!" Hermit was shouting, pulling at his hair. "Not while I'm in charge!"

Mira dashed out of the cage, stumbling on legs stiff from sitting for hours. At the wall, she grabbed the wand, slipping it into her sleeve.

Sara was behind her, pulling down a huge sword—she could barely heft it.

"Weapons are illegal here," Mira said.

"*You've* got one," Sara said.

Hermit was screaming, "Klumpet! Bran!" Presumably those were the names of the bigger ogres, who Mira definitely did not want to see again.

"Let's go," Mira said.

They ran quickly through the gaping hole in the brick and out onto the avenue. Or at least Mira did. Sara was having trouble dragging the heavy sword behind her and was slower getting out.

"Leave it," Mira said.

"I don't want to," Sara said, grunting as she tugged at it. "It's the great sword of Zeebee."

"More like the Shining Sword of Stupendous Sara," Mira said. She had meant to be sarcastic, but the mouthful phrase did have a sort of ring to it.

"Yes!" Sara said.

The rhino came barreling out behind them. Mira pulled Sara out of the way. The sword clattered to the pavers and was immediately trampled by the rhino's massive hooves.

"My shining sword!" Sara said. It was broken in two.

"You need a better one," Mira said, getting to her feet. "But how'd you find me?"

"Everyone knows where the jail is," Sara said scathingly. She examined the pieces of sword, trying to fit them back together.

"A mouse family told us about thee," a pixie said. A small movement and the sheen of fancy cloth; the pixies were riding up on the rhino with Beans.

"No, Claude smelled you out," Beans said. "He can smell out anything, can't you, Claude?" She patted the rhino's ear affectionately.

"How did you guys find a rhi—never mind. Thank you for getting me out. You've saved me for sure. But you need to go," Mira said. "Go to the Middleway, say 'Between,' and jump in. That'll take you back home. The wizards will probably be back any minute now."

"The Middleway?" Sara said.

"The water. It'll take you back home. You need to go back home."

"We don't want to," Sara said. "Why should you get to have all the fun?"

"I don't want to leave Claude," Beans added. "He likes us. He ran away too." The rhino snorted, seeming to agree that he didn't want to be left behind.

Good grief. Mira could not get away from them. They'd even followed her through a portal into another world! "Sara, listen to me. This place is not just fun and games. The ogres *eat* prisoners. I'm sure busting out a prisoner is going to get you into trouble too. Then they'll eat you both."

"The queen is not to be ingested!" a pixie shouted.

"Yes, the queen needs to go back to Between to keep her safe," Mira said.

"But you need to come too," Beans said. "You need to make the tacos."

Mira was suddenly infuriated. "I do not want to make any tacos!"

"Why not?" Beans said.

"Just go back!" Mira said. "Why aren't you listening to me?"

"Mira! Sara! Beans!" someone cried.

"Oh, there's Mom," Sara said. "She traded her earrings and coat to this faun to take her into the jail. You can see how well that worked. I *knew* that faun was sketchy."

Val was indeed missing her coat and earrings. Also, her pajamas were no longer so flowery; she looked like she'd fallen into a bucket of mud. She ran in their direction. "You got her! You got her out!"

Mira simply wanted to find her family. Why were Val, Sara, and Beans making this so hard? "Look, thanks for coming for me," Mira said to Sara. "But you can see I'm fine now. And you're going to be in trouble if you stay. Go back to Between through the Middleway, *please*, all of you. Right now. I've got to go!"

She dashed over to the edge of the avenue and looked down. Here, she was a good ten feet above the water level, the water itself swirling, dark, and brooding. People and creatures weren't jumping from that height. They were going down to the catwalks. It would be more practical to find a safer, lower place to jump in. And what if a squid monster, or worse, was swimming around in this part?

But Mira had to know about her grandmother. And she didn't want to wait any longer. She ignored the shouts behind her.

"Wynfarish!" she cried as she leaped.

* * *

Mira was very small. She sat in Gammy's lap. They rocked while Gammy read her a picture book. Gammy smelled of lemon soap and freshly washed sheets and biscuits baking.

"What are you looking for?" Gammy said. Her breath tickled Mira's ear.

"In the book?" Mira said. She was fascinated by the colorful monsters drawn on the page. They really seemed to be romping.

"No, Mira, what are you looking for in your life?"

Life. Death. The second always followed the first. "Stop it, Gammy. I know you're trying to trick me. I know you're imaginary. I know you're really gone."

"Am I?" Gammy said. "Hmm."

Gammy didn't *feel* very gone, Mira thought. Gammy felt soft and warm and real. Mira didn't turn around to check. She didn't want this moment to be over. She kept gazing at the book and could have sworn a monster in *Where the Wild Things Are* rolled its eyes.

"Do you know what it is?" Gammy insisted. "What it is you're looking for?"

"I do." Mira reached out to turn to her favorite page, which was even more favorite than the part with the hot supper. "Here," she said, and pointed to the words: *where someone loved him best of all.*

"Ah, I see," Gammy said. "That place. How will you know when you've arrived?"

"I'll feel it," Mira said. And it would be just like now: when she knew Gammy was there—even though Gammy couldn't actually be there—and that Gammy loved her.

"Remember that, then," Gammy said. "Remember to notice how you feel."

* * *

177

Mira gasped for breath as she emerged from the water. She was on her knees in soft silt. She rubbed her eyes, and there was a wide face with a long nose directly in front of her.

Mira flinched, startled.

The sheep merely bleated, flicking its ears.

"Why . . . hello to you too," Mira said, laughing.

She was on the bank of a slow-moving river. Other sheep were nearby, a whole herd of them scattered about, grazing or dipping their heads to drink, their wet-wool smell in the air, along with scents like licorice and freesia. A warm breeze touched Mira's cheeks, and birds chirped from what looked like thousand-year-old oaks. A field of wildflowers shimmered in shades of green, marigold, and scarlet. The sunlike star was tinged violet, and a purple moon in the sapphire blue sky seemed to loom quite close.

Yes, that was definitely an unfamiliar moon in the sky; a strange lump of a moon with coral-like ridges.

"Wynfarish," Mira breathed. "I'm really here. I must be. I've made it."

Chapter Twenty-Six

Mira waded out of the river, wringing out her hair and then her shirt. She turned her head to the side, trying to get the water out of her ear. The temperature was mild, the sun warm on her cheeks.

She wanted to sit there on the riverbank and dry out while she enjoyed the smells and the sounds and the beautiful views of Wynfarish. But she had a grandmother to find.

The wand was in Mira's sleeve. She felt its weight. She still had it and could show it to her grandmother as proof that her story was true. Everything was going to be fine. Everything *was* fine. "Hello, Wynfarish!" she cried.

The birds in the trees chirped louder, and a tiny brown bird came to land on her shoulder, twittering at her ear. The sheep bleated again, and a host of others did the same. A welcoming chorus. There was also a sheepdog, she saw now, a shaggy white animal that resembled a sheep himself. He didn't seem upset by her sudden appearance—he simply watched amiably from where he rested on a grassy knoll.

Bells or tags on the sheep might have indicated a shepherd

nearby. But there were none. And Mira's calling out resulted in no return shouts. She dumped the water out of her glittery sneakers and put them back on.

"Do you know which way I should go to find people?" she asked a sheep while retying her shoes.

Its only response was to nudge her hand for a scratch on the head.

She approached the dog on the hill respectfully. He was a dignified creature, clearly on the job and uninterested in her attentions. But when she asked him the same question, he turned to look deliberately into the woods that fronted the water, then returned to watching over his flock.

"Thank you," Mira said.

Inside the woods, trees with canopies like umbrellas raised silky leaves to the sky, their undersides a lace of branches. Other trees had periwinkle fruit growing straight out of their trunks, and still others bore leaves the color of orange sherbet. Small animals with shining fur scurried underfoot, and yellow ants the size of squirrels carried off seedpods to nests somewhere. There was no path that Mira could find. She wound her way through the trees.

She felt no fear. The animals didn't act alarmed by her presence, and everything seemed somehow familiar and just wonderful. This *must* be where her mother was from.

At a bright clearing filled with indigo flowers, Mira imagined herself with a blanket and a book. At a tree with many low branches, she pictured herself climbing and hanging by her knees. At a shady stand of trees, she imagined herself napping in a hammock. Once she found her grandmother and got settled in, there would be so many places for her to discover.

After a time of Mira happily wandering, a frog trilled from a tree nearby. With no better destination in mind, she walked toward the sound.

The frog seemed to move from tree to tree, trilling, then gurgling, then chirping. Mira *guessed* it was a frog. But she couldn't see it. And it moved fast for a frog. She followed the sounds. Finally, she noticed the dirt on the forest floor was tamped down and realized she'd stumbled onto a path. The smell of woodsmoke reached her.

She encountered a thatched hut. An elderly woman with gray curls tucked into a white cap was out front, sitting on a stool and churning butter.

"Are you my grandmother?" Mira said.

The woman laughed. "I highly doubt that, seeing as I have no children. Are you lost, my sweet? Have you come from the river?"

Mira nodded. "I came from One-Place-or-the-Other."

"Ah, I see, and you came to Wynfarish on purpose, did you?"

"Yes, I came to find my family," Mira said.

"It's not too often we have visitors here. Not a very exciting land is Wynfarish. We're behind the times, or so I'm told. But I hope you'll find what you're looking for here. Can I get you some refreshment before you follow the lane?"

Accepting food from a woman in a hut in a strange land

didn't sound like the smartest move to make. Val definitely wouldn't have approved. But at the mention of food, Mira's stomach contracted in pain. And really, accepting the food would be the smallest risk she'd taken that day. "That would be wonderful," Mira said.

"Bayless!" the woman called. And to Mira: "These old bones aren't cooperating lately. Go on inside and he'll fix you up. And don't worry. He likes to do it. It's our dear little ritual, his job, and he doesn't allow anyone else the satisfaction."

Mira walked into the hut from the front, and a brown-and-white miniature pony with a braided mane clomped in from the back. Since Mira didn't see anyone else in the small hut, she asked the pony (Bayless, she assumed) for some food, and he pulled out a cupboard drawer with his teeth. The drawer contained a grainy homemade bread and cheese wrapped in paper.

"That looks delicious!" Mira said.

The pony whinnied in delight.

"That's what I used to do, back in Between," Mira said. "I was in charge of the meals." It gave her a twinge in her chest, remembering how Val had called them "rituals" too. But now she couldn't quite recall why that had hurt so much. Val had always thanked her. "Thank you very much," Mira said to the pony.

He seemed to have been waiting for that. He nodded at her, shaking his mane.

After Mira had eaten and thanked the woman—whose name had turned out to be Mrs. Ladonna—Mira said, "You mentioned a lane?"

"It's just beyond the poplar tree there," Mrs. Ladonna said. "Do you know where you're headed?"

"No, not really. I only know my grandmother had a daughter named Aisling and, oh, and to prove to her who I am, I have this wand to show her." She took it from her sleeve.

Mrs. Ladonna cowered, palms in front of her face. And although Mira couldn't really hear the woman's shouts over the tremendous clanging-thrum coming from the wand, she immediately put the wand away again.

"I'm so sorry," Mira said. "I wasn't thinking."

Mrs. Ladonna put a hand to her chest, as if checking on her heart. "That was nearly the end of me. Oh my. What a scare. We no longer use the Wands of Wynfarish, child. The families have put them away for very good reasons. I had no inkling any of them were still out and about. But I read the signature on that one loud and clear. You're at the right place. Don't make any turns, just follow the lane. You'll want Poole. All the way at the end."

"What are the reasons?" Mira said.

"Your grandmother will tell you, I'm sure," Mrs. Ladonna said, her brow heavy.

Mira felt the woman's eyes on her as she walked to the poplar tree. When she turned to wave goodbye, the woman still wore the concerned expression. She stopped churning butter long enough to wave back.

Whatever Mrs. Ladonna was uneasy about, Mira felt sure her grandmother would explain it.

Just beyond the tree, Mira found the lane, as Mrs. Ladonna had described. It was really no more than a winding footpath that extended only in one direction. Mira set off, passing cozy cottages with goats and sheep wandering about, a few horses and cows. She noticed unhitched horse carts, but there didn't seem to be any cars. That was perfectly acceptable to Mira. She wouldn't miss cars. She could get used to walking or riding horseback to get around.

Poole, Mrs. Ladonna had said. Was that Mira's grandmother's last name or her first? Mira should have asked, though she assumed it was a last name. Mira wouldn't change hers from *Mira Blaise*, of course. *Blaise* had been Papa's name and she cherished it. But maybe . . . "Mira Poole Blaise," she said aloud. It would be a nice middle name. Maybe she could have both.

As in Between, the animals here were friendly. And there were so many to greet! The flock of geese at the corner, a doe and fawn grazing round the bend, a small, furry animal similar to a marmot, intent on some important errand—it had a delightful cheep of a hello. The people too: a man in a burgundy vest carrying a bucket of flowers, a woman in skirts hoeing her garden, a child with dark curls playing with a squatty dog. They all waved.

Mira was just returning the child's wave and not paying attention to where she was going when she nearly stepped into a pile of cow dung—a close call! If she'd stepped in that, the glittery silver sneakers would never be the same. She doubted there'd be an It's Fashion or DSW here for her to replace them.

The thought of It's Fashion gave her a twinge of guilt over

the clothes Val had recently bought for her, all of which Mira had left back in Between. But probably Sara would grow into the clothes soon, and they would completely forget the clothes had ever been meant for Mira to begin with. Mira wondered if she'd ever thanked Val for them. She remembered being upset at the total on the register and feeling like she'd lost her voice. She hadn't said anything, she realized. Mira felt bad about that now. Val *did* work hard for her money.

Out of the corner of her vision, Mira caught a glimpse of a golden bird, flying among the trees. When she looked closer, it had vanished. It was only a glimpse, but it reminded her of the bird Edwin. No need to be alarmed, Mira assured herself. It surely wasn't the same bird. Wynfarish was where Lyndame was from. There were probably any number of those birds here. But spotting the bird and being reminded of Lyndame gave Mira an uncomfortable feeling.

A chill was creeping into the air. The violet-tinged sun was lower on the horizon.

Still, the lane curved on.

Mira knew she needed to hurry. She wouldn't be able to see where she was going after dark. But she'd acquired several new and painful blisters on her feet, and the going was slow. She stumbled over some unexpected potholes.

Finally, finally, the lane dead-ended at a cottage.

The cottage was on the larger side but similar to the ones she'd been passing: window boxes, a thatched roof, and a brick chimney spewing smoke. Pots of red gardenias flanked a merry little gate that led to a front door painted seafoam green.

This must be the place. It had to be. All the way at the end.

Mira felt like she'd aged a thousand years in the last few days. If someone told her that her hair had turned gray and her face was covered in wrinkles, she wouldn't be surprised.

At the door, she took a deep breath and knocked.

No one came.

But she had traveled much too far to turn back. She knocked again and began counting.

When she reached a count of twenty, she tried the knob. The door was unlocked and swung open. "Hello? Grandmother?" Mira said. "I'm coming in!"

Her footsteps fell onto wooden planks. The furniture was stained honey brown and was covered in knitted doilies, the upholstery plump and comfortable-looking. Mira passed through a front hall, a gathering room. A fire burned low in the hearth.

Was nobody home?

The tiniest movement out the back window.

"Hello?" Mira said, and exited out the back door into a small sunroom.

A woman with gray-streaked hair in a tidy bun sat at an easel, painting in the dying sunlight. "I'd say come in, but I see you've done that already." The woman didn't sound particularly annoyed; she didn't even look up from her painting.

The woman's eyes were wide-set, her nose pinched, her mouth small. She looked very much like the picture of Mira's mother from the photograph Mira kept in her bedroom, only this woman was older.

Mira was speechless; here was the grandmother she'd been looking for, the *family* she'd been looking for, and she didn't know what to say.

"Well? What is it? Are you the new delivery girl with the eggs?" The woman finally looked up. "Some different sort of clothes you've got on there. You're not the delivery girl, are you?"

"Grandmother?" Mira said.

"She's damp," the woman said, as if she was speaking to someone nearby, "and her clothes are odd. She's about . . ." And then she met Mira's eye. "How old are you, girl?"

"Eleven."

"Yes, that would be the right age. Are you Aisling's child, come through the Middleway to pay me a visit, then? How nice. I'm Grandmother Poole." Her eyes flicked back to the painting, and she made a deliberate stroke with the brush.

"A visit?" Mira said. "Oh no. I've come to live with you. Gammy's gone. Papa's gone. You're the only relative I have left, um, Grandmother Poole."

The woman rinsed the paintbrush in a tin cup of water, clicking it against the edges, and then set it carefully on a towel. "Aisling, too, is gone?"

Mira hesitated. "Yes. She died when I was a baby."

"Ah, I see. I thought so." Grandmother Poole cleared her throat, but she wasn't looking at Mira. "Well, I suppose we can make this work. I've got an extra bed in the upstairs bedroom. Some clean quilts. You're in for the night, then?"

Mira studied her. "Why are you not more surprised? Did you know about me?"

"Yes, I did. Aisling came to see me there at the last. To tell me she was going to have a baby and wasn't ever coming back." Grandmother Poole's lips twisted, and a single tear ran down her wrinkled cheek.

"Oh! I'm so sorry to have upset you," Mira said.

"My girl, you must forgive me. Aisling was such a light in the world, such a dear, dear thing. I suspected that light was snuffed out, my heart felt it. But now to know for certain . . . You see, there truly has never been another like her, never another to compare. You should have seen her dance. She had such grace. She liked to laugh too. What a sense of humor. And her sweetness! She used to leave me these little notes. Thinking of her, I'm quite overcome."

Mira sighed. "You must have loved her so much."

"I did. So very much. She and I were so close. I miss her dreadfully." Grandmother Poole's eyes went misty.

"Don't believe a word she says," someone said from the door. It was Lyndame. "She's nothing but a liar."

Chapter Twenty-Seven

Lyndame didn't look so good. The dark makeup had smudged beneath her eyes. An angry red scratch marred her cheek. And there was a gaping rip at the knee of her pants.

At her throat was the emerald-green pendant. *Mira's* pendant.

"You're calling someone *else* a liar?" Mira said.

"I knew you'd get here eventually," Lyndame said. "You should leave while you still can."

"I'm not going anywhere," Mira said. "I live here now."

"Yes, with you, Lynnie," Grandmother Poole said mildly. "I'm putting her up in the room with you. So, hush all this nonsense."

"What?" Mira said. Lyndame was *living* here?

"Never mind that," Lyndame said. "I read her diaries, *Mother*. I've just finished. I found them under the floorboards last night. She'd *hidden* them. Why would she need to hide her diaries, do you think?"

"Whose diaries?" Mira said.

"Always with the drama," Grandmother Poole said. "You've

always had enough to eat, a good education, clean clothes. Why do you insist on such drama?"

"You didn't love her the way you describe," Lyndame said. "Nothing she did was ever good enough. You made her miserable! Why do you think she never came back?"

"Are you talking about my mother? Are you talking about Aisling?" Mira said. What was happening? This was all going very wrong.

"Ah, my dearest Aisling," Grandmother Poole said. "She was the good girl in the family. Always so quick in school, so clever. Always so cheerful. She had such control of her emotions, such discipline. My beautiful Aisling."

Lyndame put fists to her ears. "Stop it, stop it, stop it. Why do you keep talking like that?"

"Why should I not?" Grandmother Poole said. "Why should I not talk about my wonderful daughter. I miss her each and every day."

"But you don't. You criticized her clothes, her hair, her speech. She had a stutter because of you—for years. It's all written down!" Lyndame said.

"Children frequently misremember," Grandmother Poole said. "Much like a certain someone I know. But come now, we have a guest. Is this the proper way to treat a guest? Aisling would never have behaved this way. She would have put on a clean shirt, at the very least. My goodness, I can smell you from over here."

"You're being critical again. You are! You can see it, can't you?" And Lyndame was asking Mira that part. She was looking Mira's way.

What she saw wasn't right, that was for sure, Mira thought. The way Lyndame was acting. The way her grandmother was acting. It was all wrong. Mira was supposed to find her family, her *true* family. This was going to be where she would live, forever and ever. But Lyndame had taken Mira's pendant, stolen it, the most precious thing Mira owned. And Mira's grandmother. Why . . . she was not what Mira had expected at all. Her grandmother was supposed to be happy to see her. She was supposed to be nice, caring. That was the way grandmothers were *supposed* to be.

Without Mira being quite aware of what she was doing, her hand crept to her sleeve.

Lyndame's eyes widened. "It's got more power here . . . don't—"

But the noise was already beginning. A ringing like a bell tower, resounding through the room. The floorboards rumbled beneath her feet. The paint pots on their table rattled. The windowpanes clattered in their frames.

Mira had the wand in her hand. Why didn't she put it down? She didn't want to put it down.

She opened her mouth and her voice boomed like a hundred Miras: "This is where I belong! You are supposed to love me!"

The word *LOVE* appeared in the air written in shining sparks of magic, a word that filled the room, each letter taller than Mira. Then the sparks came together to form a glittering ball the size of a basketball, as though a magnet drew them in. Lyndame and Grandmother Poole stared at the ball in horror. The house shuddered like a shock wave of thunder was running through it, and the ball drew itself tighter and tighter, smaller and smaller, until the pressure was so great, the ball of light broke into a million pieces with a tremendous splintering sound, shattering every last sunroom window.

It was as if something fundamental in the world had been unleashed. A mass of sparks fell onto Grandmother Poole and Lyndame like a horde of angry bees. The force knocked Mira backward, off her feet and onto her rear, where she slid across the floor, landing with her back against the wall. Her vision blurred.

"Oh, Papa," Mira said into the blurry world, into the continued tolling of the wand, into the swirling, thronging magic. "Why did this happen? You shouldn't have left me. You should be here with me." And as the magical sparks rushed out the windows . . . "I'm sorry, I didn't mean to . . ." But that last bit wasn't true. She *had* meant to do it, whatever she had just done. She wanted it, yearned for it with all of her heart.

A few moments later, the wand seemed to be telling her it was finished—the magic was complete. Mira shakily put the wand back into her sleeve. The sounds were gone. The reverberations stopped. The furniture was turned over. The windows were holes; only a few jagged bits of glass remained in the frames.

It was like the space of quiet after the world ends.

Grandmother Poole was lying flat on her back on the floor, her hair standing up in all directions, as if she'd been struck by lightning. But she struggled to rise, cleared her throat, and smoothed her hair, attempting to put the wild strands back into the neat bun; it didn't quite work, a few sprigs would not be tamed. When she'd gotten herself together, as best she could, she said, "Well, now, why don't we all have a spot of supper? I'm sure you're famished. I'd love to prepare you both something, my dear daughter, my dear grandchild."

"That would be lovely, Mother," Lyndame said, getting to her feet. "You are so dear to do that for us. Oh, and I love your painting of Aisling, beautiful as ever." The painting was on the floor too, the easel folded in on itself and flattened.

"Why, that is a picture of myself, when I was younger. I'm ever so flattered you appreciate it," Grandmother Poole said. "Now, for tonight, I was thinking the eggplant casserole. That seems like something Mira would like. What do you think, Mira? Extra cheese?"

Lyndame turned to her too. "Yes, Mira. We want everything to be as you like, since it's your first dinner with us. Should we make some place cards for the table? Pick some wildflowers for the bud vases?"

"And tomorrow you'll want to inspect my mother's cottage," Grandmother Poole said to Mira. "The one you inherited. You passed it on the way here; it's the little yellow one right before this one. Such a lovely place. Full of books and a beautiful view."

"Yes," Lyndame added. "She left it to Aisling, which I totally understood. I was only a toddler. Why should she have left it to me? Or the amulet of protection either? I wasn't resentful in the least. Ha ha ha. They were meant to pass to you. You were meant to have them both."

Their words were wonderful. It should have been perfect.

It was horrific.

Because their speech was stilted, their eyes wide and frightened, and their movements puppet-like and clumsy.

As Mira watched, Grandmother Poole's hands slowly lifted to her face. She stared at them in dread as if she had no idea what her own hands were about to do, as if she thought they might strangle her. Then, seemingly repulsed and dismayed by what she was doing, she pressed her lips to the tops of her fingers and blew an awkward kiss to Mira.

What had Mira done?

"Hello?" a voice called. Someone was coming from the front of the house.

And then suddenly everything *was* perfect and it *was* wonderful and Mira's heart came alive with joy. Because the new arrival was a man, slightly balding, in a flannel shirt, a hazel tree tattoo on his neck and a crooked smile that lit the room, brighter than the sun. And he was tentative, hunched just a tad at the door, as if he wasn't sure he was in the right place.

"Papa!" Mira shouted, and she ran to him and buried her face in that shirt that smelled of that piney soap he liked and his favorite gingersnap cookies and the wintergreen Tic Tacs, and his strong arms came down and around her, and finally all was right with the world. Here was Papa, he was really here, and it wasn't at all like New Mom and New Dad because Papa was real and she knew it. "Oh, Papa," Mira said. "I did this thing and maybe I shouldn't have done it, but now you're here and everything is going to be like it was and I'm just so happy."

"Little darlin', I can't understand what you're saying to me. Let's have a look at you." And Papa gently pulled Mira's face out of his flannel shirt, and his eyes were so familiar (brown irises with flecks of gold) and his cheeks familiar (he always shaved in a hurry and missed a few patches) and his crooked smile too (the left side of his lips always coming up first), but what he said next was strange and made no sense.

"It's clear I should know you," Papa said. "And I have this odd feeling that I *did* know you, up until a moment ago, but I've gotten lost, you see. I've forgotten something . . . well, I've forgotten myself actually, and I have this terrible feeling I'm not where I'm supposed to be."

"No," Mira said, eyes filling with tears. "You're exactly where you're supposed to be. You're here with me."

Papa extended his appeal to Grandmother Poole and to Lyndame, who seemed frozen in place, as if they were robots and their batteries had died or someone forgot to input instructions. "I'm lost," Papa said to them. "I was watching over something. I know I was doing that. And I must continue to watch. It's my job now, I'm sure of it, and I need to get back to it. It's very important that this item—no, it's a person, I feel sure it's a person—gets watched over by me. I'm kind of like a guardian . . . yes, that's what I am. A guardian. I can't remember where I was, but I need to get back there. Can you help me to get back?"

195

"It's me, don't you see?" Mira said, and a tear escaped. "It's me you were watching over. But now you can do it from here. Because I'm right here. You can stay with me, and life can be like it was."

Papa turned back to her, but his gaze was inward and his words came faster. "There's more of them, though, I can feel it's true. There's more of them I have to watch. I have to get back. There's so much at stake. I must get back! I must!" And he turned abruptly and dashed back through the house, the way he'd come, and Mira was running after him.

"Wait!" she called.

Papa broke out into a jog up the lane, speeding into a purple sunset. His voice was frantic as he called out to no one. He needed to get back and right this instant, he said, even though he didn't know where it was that he needed to get back to. He was so fast! Mira used to be able to run as quickly as Papa, or almost, but not anymore.

It wasn't a full minute, however, before Papa came back down the lane—he had turned around—passing Mira, headed toward the woods behind the house, and his feet were bloody because he'd somehow lost his shoes and he was saying, "I must get back! The way back must be near, it has to be, I can feel it, but I can't find it! Mama, help me!" And it was Gammy he was crying out for, because he had called Gammy that name all of his life.

But it wasn't Gammy who reacted, who collapsed in distress and shock at the lane, collapsed in a heap of horrified Mira, because Mira knew suddenly and with certainty that what she had done to Papa, and to Grandmother Poole and Lyndame, for that matter, was a Very. Bad. Thing.

And so, although she didn't want to do it, didn't want to do it in the least, she reached into her sleeve, took out the wand, and said, "I take it back. Put everyone back the way they were."

The sounds of bells came again, and Mira's ears hurt from hearing the bells and the vibrations from them, and right then and there she decided that she never wanted to hear them again for as long as she lived.

The word *BACK* rose large and glittering in gold and silver, and then the sparks of magic came together to open a door right in the middle of the air. A brilliant light shone out of the door, a light that eclipsed the purples and golds of the sunset.

Papa, dear Papa, sighed and said happily, "Ah, here is the way. Thank you. Thank you so very much." And he walked at once through the doorway.

The door shut behind him and the light went out.

He was really and truly gone. And the knowledge was like a knife twisting in Mira's chest, the pain so sharp it took her breath away.

"Goodbye, Papa," Mira whispered.

She threw the wand, into the woods, as far away from her as she could.

Chapter Twenty-Eight

"The Pixies" (excerpt)
'Tis said their forms are tiny, yet
    All human ills they can subdue
Or with a wand or amulet
    Can win a maiden's heart for you;
    And many a blessing know to strew.
—Samuel Minturn Peck

Mira was lying on the ground along the narrow lane when the thumping started.

The back of her head felt wet. She might have been lying in a mud puddle, but she didn't move, because what did it matter? And she didn't even look up to determine the source of the thumping because she couldn't muster up the slightest amount of concern about it.

The colors the setting sun made in the sky were beautiful in Wynfarish, she thought idly, different from Between, more bluish, but just as pretty, lighting up that purple moon that appeared to be so close by but yet was probably very far away.

She really didn't care about that either.

"Mira!" *Miwa.*

Ah, so it was Beans. Of course it was Beans. Beans was likely the only four-year-old in all of existence who would have been able to follow Mira to Wynfarish. How about that. Wasn't that amazing. But why was Beans thumping?

The slightest bit of curiosity stirred Mira, and she turned her head and saw that it was Claude. The woolly rhino's hooves were doing the thumping. Riding on his back were *all* of them: Val, Sara, and Beans, somehow still wearing her crown.

Well, that wasn't a sight you see every day. The rhino's long, yellowish hair looked purplish in this light, Mira thought. Lavender, maybe. A big, fluffy, lavender rhino with three people on his back. She almost giggled, and she would have, if she'd had the energy.

Val jumped down, still wearing those filthy and ridiculous pajamas, and ran over to Mira. "Can you move?" Val said.

"Yeah," Mira said, although she didn't, and she felt Val's hand on the back of her head, and then on the small of her back, helping her sit up.

"What's happened? Why are you lying out here? What's wrong with you?" Val said.

"Papa's gone. He's dead," Mira said, and burst into tears.

Val pulled Mira into an awkward hug and patted her back and said how sorry she was, how difficult this year must have been for Mira, and repeated "There, there" a bunch of times, which really made no sense.

"Mira's crying," Beans whispered loudly to Sara.

"She'll be okay," Sara whispered back. "Stop looking at her."

Mira kept crying because she couldn't seem to stop. She also couldn't put her arms up, couldn't hug Val back, and she didn't know why. After a long time, she sniffled. "How did you know I was here?"

"I heard you say the name!" Sara interjected. "And we decided to come too. It was all because of me."

"Claude sniffed you out," Beans said. "Claude knew where to go."

"No, it's because *I* knew where to go," Sara said. "Stupendous Sara to the rescue!"

"Claude! Not *Stupid*-ness Sara," Beans said.

"The queen is always exactly correct!" a pixie said from atop the rhino.

And then they were all arguing.

Good grief, Mira thought. The pixies had come in riding on Claude too. "Claude needs to mind his own business," she said.

Beans and Sara and the pixies were too busy arguing to hear. The rhino snorted, as if *he* had heard and disagreed about what was his business.

Mira waved Val away and got to her feet, a trifle unsteadily. "I'm okay now. I have a house here, I found out. A cottage. It's mine. It's just for me. With books in it. And a view. So, I'm going to be fine in my new life."

"Your new life? Here? All by yourself?" Val said.

200

"Why did you come?" Mira said. "Why did all of you come here?"

"You're my responsibility," Val said. "I couldn't let anything bad happen to you. Your dad wanted me to take care of you."

"Your *responsibility*?" Mira said. "You came into another world to find me because I'm your *responsibility*?"

"Well, to be perfectly honest, I thought you were drowning. I would have dressed better if I'd known where we were going." Val laughed, but it didn't sound like she actually found it all that funny.

"But . . . that was only the first passage. You had to come *here* from One-Place-or-the-Other, didn't you?"

"Yes, of course, Sara and Beans insisted," Val said. "Though we did have Claude with us for protection."

"But you didn't have to let them have their way, did you?" Mira said. "You had to jump into the Middleway to come here. You did that part on purpose. What does that mean?"

Mira was studying Val in confusion and frustration, and suddenly it seemed like a younger Val—a more vulnerable and uncertain Val—was peering out through Val's eyes. It reminded Mira of how Sara had looked when her smile had slipped after school that day. Mira felt her heart move in her chest, and something between Mira and Val shifted. Mira realized she had forgiven Val for the day Papa died, forgiven Val for not thinking of her, for leaving her at the gymnastics meet. Val had made a big mistake, but Mira made big mistakes too.

They spoke quickly at the same time:

Mira said, "I need to tell you what happened with Papa, it was awful—"

Val said, "This isn't the best place to talk, but I didn't want to push you—"

"Mira!" came a shout from the house. And Grandmother Poole was marching out to them. "How dare you! How dare you use magic for that!"

Mira and Val stopped talking. Sara and Beans and the pixies hushed. Even Claude backed up a step.

"Excuse me," Val said, and her eyes were like blue flint as she drew herself up tall (though truthfully, her height was not particularly impressive). "Just what is going on here? What is it you're so angry about?"

"This . . . child . . . used magic to control my actions! It is the lowest and most despicable use of magic there is. Aisling must be turning over in her grave. Her daughter has turned out to be a horrendous excuse for a human being."

"That is certainly not true," Val said. "But do you mean to say she's controlling you now? She's forcing you to act so rudely?"

"I didn't mean it," Mira said in a small voice. "It was a mistake."

"Then you should apologize," Val said.

"I'm very sorry, Grandmother Poole," Mira said.

"That's your *grandmother*?" Sara said, abashed.

"Not good enough, I'm afraid!" Grandmother Poole said. "I don't know if I'll ever recover from this."

"You've been injured?" Val said. "Should we get a doctor?"

"Obviously not," Grandmother Poole said, brushing imaginary dirt from her arms.

"Then I suggest we talk about this more respectfully," Val said.

"Respectfully smectfully," Grandmother Poole said. "Hard to be respectful when a child has willfully stolen dangerous magic from under lock and key, where it was kept secure for very good reasons!"

"I did use the magic, and I shouldn't have," Mira said. "But I didn't steal it. The person who stole it was—"

"It's mine! I found it!" Lyndame shouted. And she was there, with a gleeful expression, sunlight flashing on her plum braid, Edwin winging in to land on her shoulder. She had the wand, and the sound of the bells had started, and the earth beneath their feet shook like an earthquake. "I've got the amulet too! You can't touch me!"

"No, Lynnie!" Grandmother Poole said.

"It's terrible to use it," Mira said. "You'll be sorry!"

"No, I won't!" Lyndame said. "I thought it would hurt her if you died. I see now that nothing will hurt her, but I also know, thanks to the diaries, that Aisling knew exactly what she was doing, exactly what she was leaving me with. She saved herself and left me to rot! You deserve this even more than I thought, in her place. Goodbye, Mira, and good riddance!"

And there were sparks in the air and they spelled out *DEATH* and they flew Mira's way, but . . .

. . . Val threw herself in front of Mira.

So . . .

Chapter Twenty-Nine

The wand couldn't make anyone love Mira, not really. It also couldn't bring back those who were gone, today loving Mira from the ever after. The wand couldn't do all that much when it came right down to it, not actions of any true importance.

But there were those who loved Mira, here. Maybe they weren't the ones she had wanted, but they *did* love her, and they had shown her that love by following her here, rescuing her again and again. And it hadn't taken magic to make them love her. Mira finally knew that, realized it, admitted it to herself, but . . . was it too late?

Mira had fallen. Val's body was a deadweight, bearing down on Mira, and she gently moved her off and turned her onto her back. Val's eyes were closed. She didn't seem to be breathing; her lips were tinged with blue.

Mira's could feel her own heart thudding in her chest. "Are you okay? Please be okay. Please be all right, Val. Please. Please. Please."

But Val did not look okay. She did not look all right.

Beans said, "Momma?" and Sara burst into tears.

It hurt too much to love people, Mira thought. Way too much. And she hadn't wanted to do it, she realized. Because when they left you behind, your heart broke. But the truth was this: Mira loved anyway. She was full of love. Because even though Mira didn't want it to be so, was afraid for it to be so, she felt the love inside her seeping out, pouring out, flooding out; she couldn't keep it in. It cascaded down her cheeks in a soundless stream, and tears dripped from the bridge of her nose.

The more people you love, the bigger your heart gets. Before Papa had proposed to Val, he'd said that to Mira. He promised her it was so. She didn't listen much then, and hadn't thought about it much since. But it came to her at that moment: she knew what his last words meant. Val *had* gotten them right. *It gets bigger.* He meant his heart and he meant Mira's heart too. Because he'd known Mira needed to hear it.

Sara was still crying and Beans started to wail. "Nooooo. Momma!"

And then the pixies were there, surrounding them, the entire dozen who had apparently come with Claude too.

"Be well, oh queen," Hipple said. "Thy mother yet lives. We will show thee." And he motioned to a pixie in a taffeta gown.

The gowned pixie nodded and emptied her little bag of pixie dust onto Val's chest.

A long moment . . .

Val's body spasmed. She gasped for air and coughed.

"She's okay!" Mira cried, and Beans leaped onto her mother in joy.

"Beans . . . too heavy . . ." Val croaked, and Beans had to get up.

Then Beans and Mira and Sara laughed and they all crowded around Val, and the purple moon in the sky turned a glorious shade of amethyst with the setting sun.

Grandmother Poole said, "What a relief. What a day. I suppose the spell didn't quite work because of that interference. I do believe I need a cocktail."

Lyndame had moved closer, watching them together, and she said, "This isn't fair. This isn't right. Mira shouldn't be here. She shouldn't get to be happy. This isn't the way it's supposed to be!" And Lyndame was reaching for her sleeve and she was going to bring out the wand again. Because Lyndame's heart was broken and she didn't know what to do about it, Mira knew.

"Stop this bad behavior at once, Lynnie!" Grandmother Poole said.

"Lyndame, I understand how you're feeling," Mira said. "You've been treated unfairly, it's true. I know that now. She hasn't been good to you. But you're still my aunt, don't you see? We can be family, even if we're not so perfect, we can be family to each other."

Mira's suggestion shocked Lyndame to her core, that was clear. And something in her expression wavered, and there was the tiniest gleam of hopefulness in her eye, the smallest hesitation, but then she set her jaw and those amber eyes flashed. "Never! I *hate* you, Mira Blaise. Aisling chose you over me and I will never, *ever* forgive you for that!" And even though she didn't bring out the wand, didn't do any more damage in that moment, she turned and ran, Edwin flying and screaming behind, and she was taking the wand and the amulet with her.

"She won't get far," Grandmother Poole said. "Because of this hubbub, the Commission will realize she took our family's wand from the vault and they'll apprehend her. Now . . . time for that cocktail." And she brushed off her hands and was setting out for the house.

"What will happen to her?" Mira said.

"How should I know?" Grandmother Poole said without looking back. "This has never happened, not since the reckoning when the wands were put away. But she'll be stopped."

Mira could have asked then about the Commission, about the reckoning. She could have asked: *Why were the wands put away?* But she didn't. There would be time to find out later. And also—she believed she already knew why the wands would need to be put away.

She turned her eyes to where Lyndame was disappearing into the shadows of the woods. What Mira thought was this: Lyndame needed the protective amulet more than Mira did. Because even though Lyndame had said, when she'd first appeared out of the woods, that Mira was lost and alone with no parents to protect her, it was actually Lyndame who was alone, with no one but herself to depend on.

Mira turned back to Val, who was breathing better, and Mira was helping her up, and it was very much like Val had done only

208

a few minutes prior, helping Mira up from the ground.

Maybe it wasn't such a bad thing, Mira thought. This helping each other.

✳ ✳ ✳

The next day, Mira, Sara, Val, Beans, and Claude stood on the bank of the Wynfarish River. The sun shone brightly. Everyone had slept long at Mira's lovely cottage and then enjoyed a meal with Mrs. Ladonna and Bayless. Mira had leafed through her mother's diaries. Though they were sometimes difficult to read—her mother's childhood was far from perfect—Mira finally had something more of her mother, a more complete image, to hold close to her heart.

It had been a long couple of days. They were ready to go.

Well, all except for Claude. His great head hung low, coating his chin hairs with sand.

"You've gotta go home, Claude," Beans said. "I know your family was being bad, but you need to tell them they need to be on their best behavior and *no yelling*." The rhino was apparently the smallest of his family and had run away because he was getting picked on and forced out of the best grazing spots. Mira couldn't imagine how Beans knew all that, but she seemed very certain.

The rhino waded into the water, turning back toward them several times. Each time he turned, they all waved.

"Bye-bye, Claude! I'll love you forever!" Beans shouted.

The rhino finally disappeared into the water.

"Are we ready?" Val said.

They all held hands.

They were leaving the pixies behind. The group of them were settling in at Mira's cottage. She had told them they could live there so long as they allowed her, Sara, Val, and Queen Beans, of course, to come back and visit. The pixies had been very pleased and since announced they would be renovating the kitchen to better accommodate their needs for ballroom dancing and feasting.

"Will we forget?" Sara said to Mira. "When we get home, will we forget all this? Will it seem like a dream?"

Mira thought about it. In the Between Grocery, Miss Liu and Mrs. Martha had been whispering about a *secret* to be protected. They were talking about Glass Pond, she felt sure. "I don't think so. There are other people who know."

"Yes! Stupendous Sara returns from her latest adventures!" Sara yelled.

"Between," Mira said firmly. "We all need to say 'Between, Georgia.' Don't want to end up anywhere strange." She cut her eyes at them.

They all laughed. It didn't get much stranger than One-Place-or-the-Other, or at least Mira hoped not. Maybe this way they could all go straight to Between. Mira had had enough of travel for a while.

"Go home!" Beans said, and she was pulling the rest of them into the water.

Life wasn't exactly as Mira had wanted it to be, she thought as she followed.

But maybe everything would be all right.

Chapter Thirty

There was no more Mrs. Sutter.

Or more precisely, Mrs. Sutter had returned to being just a neighbor and not a babysitter. Val made Mira go over and apologize for the tricks she and Hipple had played on Mrs. Sutter when Mira was little—apparently, Hipple *continued* to play tricks on Mrs. Sutter for years, and the woman suspected Mira all along and blamed her for her stress headaches (which explained some things). Val still wasn't budging on babysitting, though, and she'd found a local high school student, Ronnie, to watch them over the summer. But Ronnie could *drive* them places, which felt like a miracle.

Neither Mrs. Sutter nor Ronnie were in attendance at the special party that Sunday afternoon in July, the gathering in Mira's backyard.

Miss Liu was there, sitting in a folding chair with an iced lemonade. The kids had spent some time at her apartment pool this summer, and she had taken the afternoon off from the library especially for this celebration; she was the new boss there as Mrs. Bongle had retired, and Miss Liu could do as she liked. Shanice was there too. Mira had invited her. Shanice had shown up with little pliers and dustcloths to work on Fairy Village, saying she missed doing that, which made Mira smile. Even Mira's sort-of friend Dublin from Loganville Middle was there. He brought a Hermione Granger bobblehead doll as a gift for Mira. The doll held a wand, which Mira found ironic.

Mira poked skeptically at a kebab—tomato with avocado—on her paper plate.

"Give avocados a chance," Val said. "Beans loves them."

Well, everybody knew that. Beans insisted on having them every taco night now. Mira was more interested in the fried chicken and biscuits Val had picked up from the Between Grocery for today's picnic. "Here's what *I* want," Mira said, reaching inside the fragrant bag to fill her plate.

Val inspected her vegetable garden. She had cleared out the weeds and recently put in some tomatoes, which she had labeled *Blaise Couch Tomatoes*. There was also *Strive for the Pole Beans* and *Doesn't Suck Squash*.

Caw! Bandit was in a tree nearby.

"Don't forget, no straws or sticks!" Mira said. Well, she had warned them. If anyone got swooped on, it would be their own fault.

"Howdy, all!" It was James the handyman, walking around from the front of the house, minus his toolbelt.

"What's *he* doing here?" Mira said. "We're fixing something *today*?"

Val's cheeks flushed pink. "No, he's just here to celebrate

with us. Not a big deal. It's nothing. Just a friend I invited."

"Come to the table!" Beans called.

It was not a table. It was a striped picnic blanket and three beach towels spread out on the grass. Beans had indicated where everyone should sit by painting their names on various rocks. No one mentioned that the *s* in Beans's own name was painted backward.

Settling into her spot on a beach towel, Mira idly pointed and flexed her feet. She and Sara did gymnastics clinics on Saturdays now. It wasn't as fun as the competitive gymnastics, but they both enjoyed it, plus the teacher often got Mira to demonstrate various moves.

She tossed a few peanuts to Bandit, then took a tiny nibble of avocado. She definitely liked fried chicken better than avocados. Mira was only able to take two bites of chicken, however, before Sara started jumping and down.

"Time for the presentation!" Sara said.

"It's not a presentation," Mira said.

But Sara insisted on parading around with the paper entitled *Adoption Petition*, which was what they were celebrating. Then they all made a big deal of signing it, Dublin too, even though it really only needed to be signed by Val.

Then everyone was looking at Mira and smiling.

Nothing was really going to change, Mira knew. She was still going to call Val, *Val*, and they were going to live there and keep their belts tightened and maybe even more so because Val had started online school to become a dental hygienist, which had surprised everyone; she said she decided if she was brave enough to follow Mira to Wynfarish, she was brave enough to go back to school. Mira was going to go back to Loganville Middle in the fall and would just have to figure it out.

No, nothing much was going to change.

At the same time—everything had changed.

Mira put down her plate. "Check us out. Come on, Sara." She dropped into a handstand, turning the world upside down, and walked on her hands. She could see Sara behind, copying her; her hand walking was getting better. And Beans was back there too, although Beans was actually walking on all fours and occasionally sticking out one leg or the other, only pretending to be walking on her hands. No one pointed that out.

"Nice and straight," Shanice said. "You've still got it, Mira-boo."

"Work it, work it," Dublin said.

"Don't give yourself a stomachache," Val said.

After walking clear across the yard to Fairy Village, the three of them dropped back to their feet.

"Ta-da!" they said, and bowed to the applause.

And that was that.

There was more for Mira to learn, more to find out about Wynfarish, more to figure out about her own life, really.

But for now, Mira had found the place where she belonged.

And it was right where she had started from. In Between.

Acknowledgments

I am so very grateful to the many people who helped bring this book to life.

Amy Cloud, my brilliant editor, for her sure-footed guidance and encouragement in developing Mira's story.

Josh Adams, my fearless agent, for advocating for my work and keeping us all on track.

The entire team at Clarion Books for stewarding this novel through the process with such professionalism and startling talent.

Anne Ursu, whose invaluable feedback helped me find the heart of the story and who continues to be a supportive influence in my writing.

Jo Hackl, whose thoughts on this story helped strengthen Mira's journey and whose generous marketing tips have been priceless to this clueless newbie.

Bralie Branan, Kinla Nelson, and Austin Moon, for their early reviews of the manuscript and incredibly helpful feedback.

The Hamline MFAC community, for their support.

This book is really my ode to family, however you find it or define it. My family's support and encouragement and love are what keep me going day after day. I can't thank them enough.